OLLIE'S WEEKEND

Book Two of Ollie's Heart

Mark Mortland

7th Street Dreams

DISCLAIMER

Ollie's Weekend is a work of fiction intended for an adult audience. It contains themes of self-discovery, LGBTQIA love, and erotic intimacy between consenting adults. While the story explores emotional and physical connections, it is written with the goal of portraying relationships with authenticity, heart, and respect.

All characters, events, and places are fictional or used in a fictional context. Any resemblance to real persons, living or deceased, is purely coincidental. This book does not depict non-consensual or exploitative situations - every romantic and intimate moment is based on trust, mutual desire, and care.

Additionally, this story touches on themes of overcoming past hardships, self-acceptance, and healing. While it includes moments of vulnerability, its core message is one of hope, love, and finding one's place in the world.

Table of Contents

Chapter 1: Whataburger

Chapter 2: The Journey Home

Chapter 3: When Ollie Met Corey

Chapter 4: An Intimate Nap

Chapter 5: A Family Hug of Acceptance

Chapter 6: A Texan Home

Chapter 7: Under Texan Stars

Chapter 8: Fathers Know Best

Chapter 9: Bad Pup, Fun Pup

Chapter 10: Nightmare

Chapter 11: Our First Morning

Chapter 12: Meet the Dads

Chapter 13: Shut Your Door, Corey

Chapter 14: Solving a Hard Problem

Chapter 15: On the Path Together

Chapter 16: Summit Declarations

Chapter 17: Forest Play Place

Chapter 18: Busted

Chapter 19: Celebrations - Family Style

Chapter 20: Revelations

Chapter 21: Movie Night

Chapter 22: Breakfast in Bed

Chapter 23: Morning Plans

Chapter 24: Dallas Attitude

Chapter 25: The Promised Land

Chapter 26: Thunderstorms and Pizza

Chapter 27: The First Verse of Us

Chapter 28: Ollie's Heart

Epilogue: Our Song

CHAPTER 1: WHATABURGER

"Ollie, I swear I'm going to try my best not to father you too much. I'm sure Dad and Ted will take charge of that. I mean, believe me, I want you to be my *boy* - but not *exactly* in a paternal way." Corey's mischievous grin softened just a bit as his concern took over. "But, seriously, when was the last time you ate?"

I glanced up from my completely demolished plates

of Sam's Benedict with a pancake side, smiling sheepishly. "Corey, this little diner is amazing. The Texas version of eggs Benedict rocks. Sausage instead of Canadian bacon? Genius. And these pancakes? To borrow your phrase, they're like 'breakfast candy.' It's just that I couldn't eat last night. I was too nervous about this morning... and about sleeping in a strange parking lot. Thankfully, I was surrounded by three really sweet RV families. As soon as I parked, they all introduced themselves and made me feel safe. I slept way better than I expected."

I hesitated, glancing away from his eyes before adding, "Anyway, I know I may be homeless, but I'm not going hungry." Then, tentatively meeting his gaze again, I continued with a more positive tone. "Did you know that Starbucks has the most amazing breakfast sandwiches? Some are even low-fat and high-protein. I can't afford their coffee all that often, but dang, those sandwiches start my morning right. And lunch is usually on the cheap in the cafeteria at work. Thursday is enchilada day." I gave Corey my goofiest "yum" face, hoping to lighten the mood.

"Weekends can be rough, though. And I also mess up a lot after my real job is over and before my LA Fitness work begins. That's when I miss home-cooked meals the most. I'm honestly a pretty good cook; my grandma taught me well. There just isn't a lot I can do in my Bronco before starting my nightly janitorial career. So, dinner is usually just me grabbing a couple chicken sandwiches at Wendy's."

I stopped, suddenly somehow worried I'd said too much. Sure enough, Corey's expression had shifted to one of quiet sadness. His look made me want to take him in *my* arms and comfort *him* - an ironic thought given the circumstances. Still, I couldn't stand seeing him upset.

So, what did I do? I apologized... "Corey, I'm sorry," I said quickly, my voice soft. "I didn't mean to upset you. I'm doing alright - *really*. I swear I even had more defined abs before I started fending for myself in my Bronco 24x7. I'm definitely not starving... I'm just not eating as clean as I should."

Corey shook his head, his voice gentle but firm. "Ollie, that's not it. It's just... someone as amazing as you - someone I'm falling for - shouldn't have to figure out how to eat properly because they're living out of their car." He tried to smile, but his eyes still held a hint of sadness. "But," he added, his grin nearly turning mischievous again, "do me a favor. If you ever tell that story to Dad and Ted, swap out Wendy's with Whataburger. You'll earn points with both of them."

I didn't quite get the joke, but I couldn't help but laugh. Most importantly, Corey was holding my hands again, looking into my eyes with an intensity that made me feel weightless. For three months, I'd been living on perpetual alert, starting every morning as if it could be my last normal day. But in Corey's gaze, I was suddenly thriving. I was happy in a way I hadn't been in a long, long time.

Our motherly waitress caught our hand-holding

moment and gave us both a satisfied smile. I think we actually just made her day. "You boys were hungry. Can I get you anything else?"

Corey started to reply but then shot me an inquisitive look. I shook my head, and he continued, "No ma'am, just the check."

She looked at me, winked, and gave me a motherly smile. "Are you okay with this guy? I have a feeling his intentions may not be the most honorable."

"Ma'am, this man just convinced me to order 'Sam's Benedict.' I think I'm safe. Besides, I know his father and, um, *uncle*. I'm good." She laughed and spontaneously leaned down to hug me. My lurd, what a day. She walked away with Corey's credit card and, I swear, with a little spring in her sway.

Poor Corey gave me a look of feigned shock and hurt and said, "Ollie, my intentions are very noble." He grinned but then rolled his eyes. "But I'm a bit embarrassed. Um, have you ever given the perfect story-ending speech and then realized the writer was an idiot? Like he didn't understand the story wasn't over yet?"

"Wait, and you say *I'm* the one who always has an internal monologue going on?"

"I will smack your bottom again, young man." I love this man's smirks. "I was talking about what I told you - *out loud* - about you living in my old room at Dad and Ted's house. But guess what? My key to their house is at *mine*. And Dad and Ted won't be at home until after five. Would you be willing to risk your maidenhead and follow me to my house for the afternoon?"

"I have no idea what my maidenhead is, but do I get to see you with your bottoms off?"

"Maybe."

"Then yes, please!"

Corey told me to put another address into my phone and then summarized our trip to make sure I wouldn't get lost on our next journey. "Ollie, we're going to take I-30 through downtown Fort Worth, then head south on University Drive. I live really close to TCU. Once again, my oh-so-beautiful boy, I do not want to lose you. Are you ready for another 45-minute drive?"

"I am. How's the charge holding up on your Mach E?"

"Are you into Mustangs?" Corey asked, raising an eyebrow.

"My dad used to tell me how my mom made him give up his brand-new GT when I was born. He had to trade it in for something more *family-friendly*. Once I was old enough to understand his sacrifice, we both mourned that car's passing. I love your car, man. I can't wait for you to give me a ride."

"I can't wait to give you a ride either." Corey's smirk was laced with playful innuendo. "And it's funny - my first car really was a growling, gas-powered GT beast. But once my body finally topped out at six-six, getting in and out of it became a real pain. I was so excited when they decided to make the Mach E into a small SUV."

"Wait, you're *three* inches taller than me?"

"I guess, does it matter?"

"No, absolutely not. We hug perfectly. I just thought you were closer to six-five."

Corey grinned. "Ah, I get it now. It's a psychological thing. All six-three boys with, um, seven-inch dicks think every other tall guy can only be an inch or two taller than them." His smirk was wickedly perfect.

"No, sir. I'm happy with my height and, um, size. But I'm even happier to be in your arms with my head on your shoulder. And I swear I'm not expecting you to have any kind of dick - big or small." Oh good lurd. "Um, that came out wrong. I mean, I... crap. I expect you to have a dick. I mean... I'm shutting up." Can I just die now?

Corey fluffed my loose curls with his hand and gave me the most goofy look ever. His easy laughter washed all my embarrassment away. "Hey, if you promise not to tell Dad... I have a special way to get to my house from I-30. I think of it as my little slalom track, and it's so much more fun in the Mach E. I promise to let you drive it. If you want to."

"Corey. I only know your dad as a kind, bearded, caring, really attractive urologist. Good lurd, now that I think about it, I'm suddenly grateful he never saw me naked. So, anyway, there's no way I'm going to tattle on my new, um..."

"Let's say 'co-explorer,' my Ollie. Mapping out our new journey together. And guess what? He was actually supposed to give you that rectal and prostate exam. I could do it since I'm a nurse and not just a normal tech. I just usually don't have to. I have no idea why he didn't, but I'm really glad he let the job fall to me."

He glanced at his watch. "Hey, we need to get to my place. It's just after noon, and the traffic should be light. I won't show you my race track this trip, but I'd love to show you my place. You ready?"

CHAPTER 2: THE JOURNEY HOME

I once again followed behind Corey's light blue "chariot of my Norse God" as we entered Fort Worth. Driving into the city on I-30 from the east, you get an amazing view of downtown as the freeway descends into the Trinity River valley. It's like the city's "hero shot," with all its glass and steel buildings gleaming in welcome. The first time I saw it - alone and afraid, right after New Year's Day - that view gave me hope. Hope that I'd be alright in this new city.

We exited onto University Drive South, heading into one of the most beautiful parts of town. Big trees lined the streets, their branches arching overhead like a green cathedral. The zoo was on the left, and Colonial Country Club was on the right. Their presence gave the area a sense of charm and history. So far, with my co-op work assignment and my night job at LA Fitness, I really hadn't had much time to explore my new home. All work and no play made me a horrible tourist, but hopefully, it would give me enough money to make it through another semester of school. As we went up a big hill, we entered TCU territory - a big prestigious school I regretfully knew almost nothing about.

Corey's house was in a quaint - and, as I'd eventually learn, ridiculously exclusive - 1950s neighborhood just south of TCU's football stadium and sports fields. He lives in a kind of football holy land. As a former wide receiver, I should have felt honored. But forgetting football for the moment, his home was the cutest, most charming cottage I'd ever seen. Unlike him, it was unassuming. But exactly like him, it was inviting and beautiful. The yard was perfectly manicured, its neat lines and flourishing plants showing care and precision. Also, just like him, the more I studied it, the more beautiful it became.

Corey pulled into his driveway, and I parked along the curb in front of his house. As I walked up the driveway, I couldn't help but blurt out, "Corey, dang! I love your home! I never expected to find a cute little neighborhood like this in a place as big as Texas. I think I just found another reason to crush on you today. Sorry, I know - juvenile - but I am still 19, sir."

He smiled at my lame joke and opened his arms as I got close. I stepped into his embrace without hesitation, hugging him tightly in public. But then immediately regretted it. "Corey, I'm so sorry. I mean, this is your home - um, where you live - I shouldn't have done that out here without asking if it was okay first."

"Ollie," Corey said gently, "that's exactly what my open arms were giving you permission to do. And you agreeing to accept it is the best thing ever. I think I told you earlier this morning - you adapt fast." He pulled me closer, holding me tighter, and kissed me... My second real kiss ever. My first one under a warm Texas April sun. I could get used to these skies. I definitely need to learn more about this Whataburger place.

"Ollie, may I welcome you into my humble abode?"

I grinned. "My Norse God, you really need to work on your lines." I snuggled into his embrace, refusing to let the moment end.

"Wait - 'Norse God?'" he asked, laughing.

"Corey, you're the one who figured out how much 'inner monologue' I write, right? When you ushered me into that chamber of horrors this morning, I realized you were my *Nurse* God.' But about half a second later, 'Norse God' popped into my brain, and, honestly, it fits way better. I hope you're okay with that." This time, *I* kissed *him*.

Corey smiled through my kiss and decided to take it to the next cheesy level. Without breaking our embrace, he lifted me into his arms like it was the most natural thing in the world. Somehow, he managed to unlock the front door, and, honest to god, he carried me over his threshold.

CHAPTER 3: WHEN OLLIE MET COREY

I'd love to tell you how perfectly Corey's house was decorated - how every piece of furniture was carefully placed. How the knickknacks, lamps, rugs, and artwork all complemented each other, blending into a perfect reflection of Corey's masculine taste and style. But I can't because I was forever trapped in his gaze.

As soon as he softly kicked the door shut behind us, he growled low in his throat and held me tighter for a heartbeat. Then, gentling his grip, he kept his eyes locked on mine and said softly, "Would you be upset if our waitress was telling the truth about my intentions?"

"Corey, I'd be really upset if she were wrong." I glanced away with heat rising in my cheeks - trying to hide my blush - before continuing, "And, well, I kinda saw *your excitement* through your scrub bottoms this morning." My voice dropped as embarrassment caught up to my confession. "That's what most of my inner monologue has been about while we were alone in our cars. I'm not sure what new level I'm ready for, but I'm definitely ready to be in your naked embrace."

He growled again, a sound that sent shivers down my spine, and nudged my face so that I was looking into his eyes once more. Without another word, he carried me through the house and into his bedroom, setting me gently on the bed. "*Baby boy*, let's get you out of that shirt and those pants again. Arms up!"

Immediately, he started lifting my shirt over my head, but before I could wriggle free, he paused. While my arms were still trapped in the sleeves and my eyes still blindfolded by the collar, I felt his lips gently kiss my left pit. Then, with deliberate care, he kissed and licked his way across my chest, pausing at my nipples.

The sensation was electric. It felt like there was a live wire running directly from my nipple to my dick. I've never thrown wood so fast in my life. "Corey," I managed, my voice barely steady, "please unzip my pants soon. My dick is not in a happy place."

He gave another low growl, the sound vibrating through me, and gently pressed his hand against my chest, nudging me back onto the bed. My shirt still trapped my arms and blinded me, leaving my pits exposed and sharing their musk with the bedroom - my scent entering Corey's den for the first time. The blindfold heightened everything - every touch, every sound, every shift of the air around me. My body responded instinctively, shivering and quaking under the weight of every sensation. All I could manage was a breathy, "Corey."

I felt his hand at my zipper, the tug of the fabric a tantalizing promise. At the same time, I felt the press of his still-clothed chest as he moved up my body, his heat radiating through the thin barrier of fabric until his breath hovered just above my still shirt-covered mouth.

"Do you trust me, Ollie?" His voice was a whisper, low and full of something that made my whole-body tremble.

"Yes," I stuttered, barely managing the word.

Carefully, he raised my collar just high enough to uncover my nose while still keeping my eyes hidden. Then, slowly, he teased my lips with the soft graze of his mustache and beard - not quite a kiss, but a promise. The sensation was maddeningly gentle, like the first hint of a summer storm, leaving me trembling with the anticipation of what was to come.

He began moving down my torso again, his lips making deliberate stops - lingering at my neck before revisiting my pits and teasing my hard nips. My skin was alive, every inch of it covered in goosebumps. When he paused between my pecs and kissed my little island of blond fur there, I felt my breath hitch.

"Ollie," he murmured, his voice low and reverent, "I'm going to love watching this patch expand across your chest. You're my beautiful flower, and I have the unimaginable honor of watching you bloom."

I couldn't help but chuckle softly at the line - until

Corey pinched my right nipple, sending a jolt of sensation through me. He followed it with slow, deliberate kisses down my light blond treasure trail, stopping to tease my belly button. My shivering kicked into overdrive. "I—I th-thought you n-never p-pinched your p-patient's nipple. Uh-uh-fuck. Oh, sorry. I mean frak."

"You're not my patient anymore," he growled softly, the edge in his voice making my breath catch again. "Right now, you're my prey, and I'm about to dive into a feast I've been craving since early this morning." His hands left my nipple and moved to my waistband, deftly unfastening my jeans and sliding them down my thighs.

He stood up from the bed, raising my legs slightly, and removed my right shoe and sock. I gasped as his tongue traced a slow, deliberate path along the sole of my foot, slipping between my toes. Another ragged "Corey" escaped my lips.

"I need to imprint every part of you onto the most primal part of my consciousness, Ollie," he murmured, his voice vibrating with intensity. "There's no piece of you I can stand to leave unexplored, untouched, or un-kissed." He slipped off my other shoe and sock, then gently eased my jeans down and off my legs. My erection strained painfully against my boxer briefs; the evidence of my arousal impossible to miss. I was sure I was leaking again - even without his amazing prostate exam.

Even as it beckoned his attention, he left my aching bulge alone. Instead, he returned to the bed, kneeling beside my quivering form and finally released me from my shirt. I was allowed to see the beautiful face of my Norse God again. And again, I beamed. He gave my smile a gentle but deep kiss and climbed off the foot of bed. "My turn my boy."

He removed his shoes as he pulled his scrub top off over his head, exposing his beautiful pits and furry dark blond pecs to me for the second time today. But this time, he didn't have to stop there. He untied the strings and let his scrub bottoms fall and fuck! He was in a very strained, dark blue jock. He saw my hero worship gaze and proudly displayed the most obscenely bulging pouch I've ever seen in any locker room.

"Corey! You were in a jock all morning? I'm so glad you didn't tell me; I would have begged those scrubs off of you and gotten us both in trouble."

"It's my standard uniform. Briefs don't cut it for me when I have to be in scrubs. I just didn't expect you to make me stretch out my favorite jock so badly today. Poor thing may never be the same again. May I remove it my Ollie? And show you what big boys do with their dicks?" He seductively chuckled. Lurd, my cousin would kill me if he knew I had told that story to Corey. But I just grinned, excitedly nodding my head.

Corey freed his most private body part and stood naked before me. He calmly let me gaze upon my prize. "Corey. You're beautiful." I couldn't take it any longer I jumped off the bed and lost my underwear as I hop-skipped across the space between us.

I melted into his arms, and again was allowed to feel his bare furry chest against my still mostly smooth one. For the first time in my life, I was treated to the feeling of another man's hardon battling mine for dominance against my lower abdomen. I inhaled his scent once more and I refused to cry any more tears, but I couldn't stop my quivers.

Corey slipped back into nurse mode for just a second. "Are we okay, Ollie? I've still got you."

"I'm absolutely okay Corey. Can I, um, can I touch you?"

"You're kinda touching me all over right now." He chuckled but continued with "Yes please, it's all for you."

I backed away just a bit and looked down at our furry abs. His, just a bit more hairy and defined. I allowed my gaze to continue downward to our bushes. Mine, a bit lighter; his, a bit darker, both thick and curly. I finally let my gaze settle on my goal. His powerful cock was throbbing, leaking and towering over his pubes. It was commanding and impressive.

I gingerly moved my hand down his chest and abs until I reached his pube line. I looked at our cocks, side by side. He was just a bit longer and a bit thicker. While my dick head was just touching his pubes, his was burrowing in to mine. We both had a slight upward curve. Unlike me, he was circumcised.

I steeled my nerves and wrapped my hand around Corey's cock. It was hot. And hefty. It felt so much heavier than mine. And I could feel his heart pulsing through it. I looked back up to his face and saw pride and satisfaction in his eyes. He passionately kissed me again.

"You're doing great Ollie, but let's not jump too many levels right now. We have a whole weekend to explore. And we've already had a very big day. Let's just get back on the bed."

He laid down first and motioned for me to snuggle in to his left shoulder. His arm wrapped around me as he started stroking his pulsing erection with his right hand. He simply said, "Please kiss me my Ollie and just cup my balls with your hand." I did and I was totally enthralled as I fondled a man's testicles for the first time. I knew the inevitable was near and reveled as they eventually drew up close to his body. His kiss intensified and his arm around me pulled me in tighter. He growled into our kiss one final time as I felt his hot liquid paint our beards. I was once again so very happy that another little tear of joy made its happy way down my cheek.

I was so overwhelmed by our intimacy; I had no choice. I moved down and rested my head against his heaving chest, pressing my ear to my Norse God's heart. The steady thrum of his heartbeat and the rise and fall of his breath slowly returning to normal were all I could hear. I was mesmerized by his rhythm, by the warmth of his skin, and by his scent. I was home.

He kissed the top of my head, a soft, reassuring gesture that sealed our moment.

"Ollie, that's so beautiful but you just got your beard really messy again. I'm sorry."

"I'm not. Does this count as scenting my beard with you?"

"Aww." He gave a big grin. "Not exactly, but I love it. We just can't go out in public with that kind of scent on you." I heard and felt his giggle through his beautiful chest.

"Hey Ollie, we need to take care of you now. Once again, I think I know how. I swear to you; I'm 100 percent safe. I'm a nurse and I have to be on PrEP. Dad would shoot me otherwise, and he'll probably want you to start it as well. But right now, do you trust me to use that, well, beard gel, for a purpose I think you'll like even more?"

I gave a nearly breathless "Yes sir" and he gently lifted my head off his chest and laid me flat on my back. Then he scooped his essence from my cheek and added even more to his fingers from the load dripping down his chest and abs.

"Knees up baby boy, allow me to be your lube. Let me give you a little preview of what I hope to deliver deep inside you when you're finally ready."

Those frakking eyes. Reassuring and mischievous all at once. I had no power and even less desire to resist his offer. I raised my knees. I knew my part to play. Except I really didn't. His cummy fingers slowly sank into my formerly furry hole once again for the day. And I realized Corey's seed was entering my core.

Even so, I started my steps of our dance with my hand. His head got lower and closer to my cock and balls and to where his fingers were disappearing into my soul. I could feel his breath on my sack. And I started shivering again. He took a deep breath of my pubes and let his flat, wide, tongue bathe and warm my rising testicles. That was all it took; I immediately added my second contribution of the day alongside the little bit of Corey's that remained in my beard.

At least I didn't start uncontrollably chuckling this time. But I couldn't stop myself from blurting, "Corey, I love you." Wait! "Um, I mean, I really love what we just did." Damn.

"I know, baby boy," he said softly, giving me a knowing smile. Then he kissed me once more, his lips full of understanding and warmth.

CHAPTER 4: AN INTIMATE NAP

It turned out that Corey's house had more than just a bedroom. It had a bathroom with a shower and indoor plumbing and everything. We stepped under the warm spray together, and I let my shoulders sink back into Corey's chest. He wrapped his arms around me, holding me close as the hot water cascaded over us, washing the evidence of our fun away. My immediate - and obscene - thought was that I wished he were hard again as I instinctively ground my hips into his crotch.

He playfully nibbled my ear, sending a shiver through me, and murmured, "We need to rotate positions. I'm pretty messy too." With a reluctant sigh, we parted, and I turned to face him.

I took my time washing his chest, my hands lingering as I traced every line and curve of muscle. I explored every part of him, savoring our closeness. When it was his turn, he returned the favor with the same deliberate care. It was a close thing, but I somehow managed not to have my third orgasm of the day.

As we dried off, Corey leaned in with a playful glint

in his eye and said, "Ollie, my man, do you know what the sexiest thing is that new lovers can do on their first day together?"

"No, sir. Haven't we already done quite a lot?" I replied, matching his grin.

"This, my boy, is next level," he said, shooting me my now favorite mischievous grin. "They nap together."

I couldn't help but chuckle.

"I had to get up at five this morning to get to you on time," he added. "Bonus: Dad and Ted want to take us out to a fun dinner tonight."

Grinning back, I teased, "Hey, if you'd have asked, I could've directed you to the safest Walmart parking lot to spend the night. It's even close to a Buc-ee's, so you could've washed up in the morning."

Corey's grin faded as his hands cradled my cheeks, his touch firm yet gentle. "Never again, my Ollie. Never. Now, would you do me the honor of being my cuddle-otter while we take a little break?"

"Yes, sir!" I laughed, and we jumped naked into Corey's bed, sliding under the cool sheets. I immediately snuggled into his big spoon, feeling euphoric all over again. "Corey? Thank you. This is the first time I've slept in a real bed since leaving home. And not only that, but I get to be in it with you."

"My Ollie." I felt his smile on the back of my neck as he hugged me tighter.

It also turns out we were both more exhausted than I realized. We fell into a deep sleep - him holding me, and me surrendering to his comfort and protection.

****

I felt a gentle shake and heard Corey's soft voice. "Hey, Ollie boy. We both needed that a lot more than we realized. It's almost six, and we need to head over to Dad's."

I hadn't slept so soundly in... well, I knew exactly how long it had been. It took me several long seconds to realize Corey was no longer spooning me. Instead, he was kneeling by the side of the bed, fully dressed, his eyes warm and attentive as he brushed my curly locks gently away from my sleepy eyes.

But even with his tender touch, my instincts still took over. I bolted upright in a panic, gasping for breath as my adrenaline surged. I caught the flicker of concern in Corey's face and forced myself to calm down, murmuring my favorite words: "I'm sorry, Corey." Then quickly continued, "You're fine. It's just... anytime I've been woken up by someone recently, it hasn't been to their loving touch."

His expression softened further, and he cupped my cheek. "My brave Ollie," he said quietly. "As I told you - *never again*." He kissed me softly, his touch grounding me as my panic faded.

"I'd love to keep you naked and in my bed forever," he added with a teasing grin, "but we need to get going."

CHAPTER 5: MY FAMILY HUG OF ACCEPTANCE

I once again followed Corey's EV as we cruised along a near-by thoroughfare. The road dipped down a hill, crossed over a wooded creek before opening up into the most beautiful neighborhood I'd ever seen in Fort Worth. The broad boulevard was divided by a wide park, with the creek we'd just crossed running right through the middle. Towering trees lined the creek and shaded the immaculate front yards on either side. I couldn't believe this was Texas. It felt more like a dream.

Corey's brake lights flashed on, and his turn signal blinked as he pulled into a circular driveway in front of a stunning huge brick home, protected by the sprawling canopy of a giant live oak. My chest tightened as I parked behind him. I hadn't grown up poor - not by any means - and I'm grateful for that. Or at least I *was* grateful. But the truth is, small-town suburban Michigan isn't the same as big-city Texas. Was this really the house I was supposed to move into?

I pulled in behind Corey and turned my engine off. Then I hesitated, my hand frozen on the door handle. I wasn't sure I belonged here.

Corey seemed to sense my hesitation. He walked up to my window, bent slightly, and met my eyes. His voice was steady, full of quiet conviction. "Ollie, I can't lose you. You're home, my boy. It's okay. We're still in this together."

His eyes settled something deep inside me. I took him at his word and stepped out of my car. Corey immediately wrapped his arm around my shoulders, his steady presence reassuring me as he guided me toward the front door. The scene was golden in hue, the magical twilight hour casting everything in a warm glow as Corey's father - my urologist - and my work mentor, Ted, appeared in the open doorway and stepped out to greet us.

Corey shouted as we approached, "Dads! I found the cutest stray puppy this morning, and he followed me home. Can we keep him?"

I froze, torn between wanting to slap him or hug him. It was seriously a toss-up.

Before I could decide, Dr. Rainer - no, Chris - was the first to speak. "Hey, Ollie, it's great to see you again. I'm so sorry about keeping secrets from you. I hope Corey helped you through your test this morning."

"Yes, sir, he did," I replied earnestly. "And I appreciate all the thoughtfulness you all put into this. I'm sorry I was too scared to ask for help on my own."

I guess something about what I'd just said, triggered Ted to jump in. His warm voice was somehow cutting as he stepped closer. "Ollie, I'm afraid I need your middle name, son."

Out of the corner of my eye, I barely caught Corey giving me a very comical "Don't do it, Ollie! Danger! Danger!" look and hand movements. But I just missed his cue, and true to form, I did what I do best: I respectfully responded, "It's Aaron, sir."

Corey put his hand over his face and waited. Uncle Ted was now armed with everything he needed, and he wasted no time before using it. "Oliver *Aaron* Carson! Sport! What the heck have you been thinking? Sleeping in your car? In dangerous parking lots? Not asking anyone for help? Getting beaten up and hurt?" He tilted his head in a serious, fatherly way and finished with, "I know you're smarter than this, Oliver."

It was only a gentle rebuke, but it still blindsided me. Thankfully my ever-present protector stepped in immediately, gently nudging me into his dads' opening arms.

They both wrapped me in their embrace just as my tears made yet another stupid appearance for the day. Corey broke the silence with his usual charm. "Dads, you made my pup cry again. He does that a lot; I think he might be broken."

I felt Chris' arm lift off me as he motioned to Corey. His mildly rebuking look was unmistakable as he said,

"Then get your butt over here and help us squeeze him back together."

And Corey did. I was completely wrapped in the arms of people who now seemed to want me.

Corey was the only one who could speak the next line. "Hey, my Ollie, I know it's not the one you expected, but can this be your hoped-for Family Hug of Acceptance?"

I looked into Corey's eyes, my heart too full for words. Encased in the arms of my new dads, safe for the first time in forever, I felt brave enough to lean in and give my co-explorer another kiss.

CHAPTER 6: A TEXAN HOME

Our kiss continued until Chris finally chuckled and said, "Okay, boys. We love you both, but get a room. Um, Corey, just not your old one - well, at least until *after* dinner." He gave us a look that explained exactly who Corey had inherited all of his expressions from. "Ollie, let's move your car around back and get your stuff in the house. We have a date with Joe tonight."

And with that, we walked into the most beautiful home I'd ever seen.

Corey picked up on his father's comment as we stepped inside. "Ollie's been here since January, but I don't think he's allowed himself to have any fun exploring his new city. I think my curly-haired pup has been too stressed and working too hard to see what our Cowtown has to offer." He reached out and ruffled the curls he'd just mentioned.

Ted, my mentor and other new dad, chimed in with a knowing look - that was just shy of making me think I'd hear my middle name again. "Ollie, did you know that co-op students aren't allowed to have secondary or part-time jobs?"

I turned to give Corey an accusing look, but before I could say a word, Dr. Rainer - Chris - cut in smoothly. "Ollie, my wonderful new son, we've already gotten your test results back."

I blinked at him in amazement. "Already?"

Chris grinned, a mischievous echo of Corey's, and said, "Hey, I'm a doctor, and my son performed the test. I have connections." But then his grin softened into a very fatherly expression of concern.

"You're a perfectly healthy young man," he continued, his tone measured and reassuring. "Except you're stressed out beyond your body's ability to cope. The guys who beat you finally pushed you over the tipping point. Ollie, you're going to have to cut back on all those extra responsibilities and just focus on being a co-op student again." He paused; his gaze kind. "But let's go to Joe's first, and we can negotiate restrictions later."

His look wasn't rebuking - it was more, well, reassuring. For the first time in a long time, I felt like someone was looking out for me, truly concerned about what I needed.

Corey led me to my new bedroom while Ted took my keys and drove my Bronco around back to a parking space by the garage. Even though the room had obviously been converted into a guest room, it still held a collection of Corey's things from throughout his life. Trophies, books, photos - each item felt like a clue to the man I was falling for. I knew I'd have fun exploring it while he was away. After all, he already knew way too many of my secrets - it was only fair I learned a few of his.

With all my meager belongings quickly stashed in Corey's former - my new - closet, my "dads" gave me a tour of the house.

It's hard to explain, but you kind of have to be in Texas to understand a Texas home. The rooms seemed endless, each one spacious and open, yet somehow still comfortable and inviting. I felt at home. Truly at home. And then they ushered me outside to the back-yard.

Their outdoor space was magnificent. Magical, even. Precisely placed landscape lighting illuminated every detail, casting a warm glow over the yard. At its center was a lagoon-style pool, shimmering like something out of a dream. The yard was nestled against the base of a tall bluff, with no visible houses above it. More live oaks bordered the space, their sweeping branches adding a sense of privacy and shade. The pool, however, was exposed, open, and waiting for the summer sun. I stood there, marveling at the beauty around me, barely able to believe that these incredible people were inviting me to live with them.

Ted interrupted my stunned silence with the most innocently incriminating question. "I know we've got Corey beat with our mature landscaping, but his new pool is going to be awesome this summer. What did you think of it?"

I froze, totally deer-in-the-headlights - for an entirely new reason. I scrambled for a response. "Um, yeah, it's gonna be great!" I blurted out, far too unconvincingly. My eyes darted to Corey for help, but he just chuckled.

Ted raised an eyebrow and tossed my weak attempt at recovery away with ease. Turning to his partner, he asked, "You've given Corey *the talk*, right?"

Corey stepped in, his voice calm and collected as always. "We were both exhausted from our early morning test and, well... we kinda fell asleep as soon as we got to my place."

Ted turned his focus back to me, his expression one of mild skepticism mixed with fatherly concern. "Uh-huh. As soon as y'all got to Corey's place..."

I felt my face heat up as I blushed furiously.

Corey, ever my defender, put a protective arm around my shoulders and said firmly, "Ted, Dad, *my* Ollie is in a very delicate and recently dangerous place. We're not doing anything he's not ready for yet."

Both men exchanged a look, their expressions softening. Satisfied, Ted and Chris gave us a pair of nods before reminding us about dinner.

"So, who's Joe?" I asked, my stomach growling; Chris' earlier comment still lingering in my head.

Chris smiled and took the prompt. "Ollie, we're about to expand your Cowtown horizons. We're going to Joe T. Garcia's Mexican Dishes. It's a Fort Worth tradition. I'm so sorry you haven't made it there yet."

Ted resumed his fatherly inquisition, his tone curious but kind. "Ollie, I know there's been at least one after work co-op get-together there. Why didn't you go?"

I looked down, the weight of past isolation settling over me. Ted's hand rested on my shoulder, his squeeze both reassuring and grounding. He exchanged a knowing look with Chris, then said softly, "It's okay, Ollie. Things are about to change for you, starting tonight. You're going to get to experience the rest of your first co-op term the way you should have been able to all along."

With that, we all piled into Chris' X5 and headed toward Joe T's, laughter and light conversation filling the car as we drove toward my new horizon.

CHAPTER 7: UNDER TEXAN STARS

Downtown Fort Worth is incredible at night. All the tall buildings are outlined with lights, like four-sided glass Christmas trees. We drove through Sundance Square, and I was in full-on tourist mode, unabashedly gawking out the windows at all the sights. For the first time, I allowed myself to relax and really-*see* it. It was wonderful. As we headed north toward the river, I felt like a kid discovering something magical that had always been right there, just waiting to be noticed.

Corey glanced over at my kid-on-Christmas-morning expression, gave my knee a quick squeeze, and said, "Ollie, we're gonna make sure you get to enjoy and fall in love with your new city. You mentioned *The Twilight Zone* this morning. Have you ever heard of an ancient movie called *Logan's Run*?"

I practically jumped out of my seat at the mention of a childhood moment with my father. "Yeah! My father and I were sci-fi nerds. I'd force him to watch the new stuff, and he'd retaliate by making me sit through his favorite old movies. Why are you asking?"

Corey grinned, clearly pleased by my reaction. "It was filmed here in Fort Worth and Dallas. When we had breakfast today, we were really close to the building they used as the Sandman headquarters - and to another office complex that was the exterior of Logan's apartment."

He paused, enjoying my shocked expression before continuing. "But tonight, we're right where Logan and Jessica swam back into the City of Domes. One of Dad's old friends was even an extra in that final scene."

My jaw dropped. "Seriously? Can we see it? I'm sorry, I mean, after we eat?"

Corey smirked. "Ask your dads." He leaned in closer, his voice dropping to a conspiratorial whisper. "Not to give too much away, but they're softies when it comes to showing off their city."

"No coaching the pup, Corey," Chris scolded lightly, though his smile softened the words as he glanced at us in the rearview mirror. "But we'll absolutely stop by the Water Gardens on the way home. Ollie, I can't believe you even know the reference. At least your dad was good for something."

Corey came to my rescue again. "Dad, let's not upset my boy anymore tonight, okay?"

We left downtown, crossing a high bridge over the Trinity River as the lights of the city shimmered behind us. Heading north on Main Street, the neighborhoods shifted - from hopeful gentrification to real Cowtown and the historic Stockyards. Turning onto an inconspicuous side street, we suddenly arrived at Joe T. Garcia's. Even from the car, I could tell why we needed to get here early - there was already a line forming to the door.

The parking lot was already half-full, lit by strands of bare bulbs strung through the trees, casting a warm glow over the cars. We hurried to join the line. The night was perfect, without a breeze, the outdoor heaters were easily able to keep the air comfortable, and the line moved quickly.

As we shuffled in, I was able to assess my first impression of Joe's. It was straight out of an episode of *South Park* - exactly like "Casa Bonita," except with a Disney-esque old Tex-Mex charm and sprawling outdoor spaces. It was utterly enchanting.

When I nervously admitted my noob status at ordering Tex-Mex, Ted just chuckled. "Don't worry, Ollie. There are only two dishes at Joe T's, and we always get the family-style enchilada dinner."

And we did. The multi-course meal was incredible, every bite a burst of Tex-Mex perfection. We sat outside by Joe's pool under more strands of twinkling lights, the warm glow adding to the magic of the evening. The four of us chattered on about everything and nothing, my new family enthusiastically trying to get to know me better.

As I looked around the table, soaking in the laughter and warmth, it hit me. Last night, I was alone in my Bronco in a Walmart parking lot, skipping dinner. Now, I was here - with Corey, Chris, and Ted - sharing a fun meal under the big stary Texas sky. I'm having a hard time believing tonight is even real.

****

As promised, after our *fabuloso* meal - I'm learning to speak Texan quickly - we visited the Water Gardens, and I recognized the place instantly from the movie. The "Active Pool" is meant to be a Brutalist abstract representation of a 360-degree waterfall, with oddly placed stepping pads leading down its cascades to a central pool 30 feet below.

Corey and I hop-stepped down the irregular pads, the rush of water growing louder with each step. At the bottom of the concrete waterfall, we were completely surrounded by roaring water, crashing down into channels that fed the churning center pool at our feet. Corey took my hand and shouted over the din, "Ready to jump in?"

From above, Corey's dads rolled their eyes. Chris bellowed down to us, his voice carrying over the roar of the falls, "Ollie, don't let our class clown be a bad influence."

Corey grinned, dodging the rebuke as he shouted back, "Ollie's a very good boy. Someone has to make sure he has a little fun." Before I could respond, he kissed me, his lips warm and reassuring even in the cool mist of the falling water.

I froze for a moment, taking it all in: I was standing in an unreal place that I'd only ever seen in a sci-fi movie, kissing my impossible new... fellow *explorer*. While less than 24 hours ago, I was homeless, with no idea what my future held. Now, I was here, in Corey's embrace, under Chris and Ted's fatherly gaze, living a moment I could never have imagined. Reality really can be stranger than fiction.

CHAPTER 8: FATHERS KNOW BEST

When we returned to Chris and Ted's house, Corey announced he was heading back to his place to grab some clothes and a toothbrush for the weekend. Before leaving, he lovingly yet sternly warned his dads, "No grilling Ollie too harshly while I'm gone." They mostly kept their word.

Ted started first, his tone kind but direct. "Ollie, damn. How you've survived this work term is amazing. I can't believe you've been able to be a superstar co-op, hold down a second job, and manage everything while living out of your car. But tomorrow, we're letting LA Fitness know that all you'll be doing at their gym from now on is working out. I know you needed the extra money, but trust me, that's no longer the case."

I opened my mouth to protest, but Ted held up a finger to shush me and continued, "It's not just me and Chris who'll be helping you out - it's your team at work too. Don't worry, your adventures are your stories to tell. I didn't give many details, but I did mention you were concerned about paying for next semester's books without your parents' support. Sport, everyone loves you. They're starting a collection, and while I don't want to spoil the surprise, let's just say your fans are being very generous."

My eyes widened, and I felt the familiar sting of tears threatening to spill over. Chris stepped in with a calm, steady voice. "Hey, Ollie, I know today must have been an emotional rollercoaster for you. And that's okay. Let those tears out if you need to - it's good for you. You seriously need to decompress. A lot of your problems look like they're coming from all that stress and worry you've built up. But maybe not all of them."

He paused, his tone shifting to something very fatherly. "I've taken the liberty of scheduling a physical for you on Monday with a very good friend of mine, a general practitioner. We need to make sure that fight didn't cause any serious damage and, well, just check to make sure the rest of you is as healthy as your bladder." He leaned in slightly, his hand resting gently on my cheek in a way that felt so familiar - so much like Corey. His smile reached his eyes as he added, "His office isn't far from here, and Corey's going to take you. You're not facing anything alone again right now. Not if we can help it."

I opened my mouth to stammer out a "Thank you, sir, but what about..." when Ted cut me off with his fatherly efficiency. "It's okay, Ollie. I know your boss." He gave me a grin that was warm enough to melt the tension from my shoulders. "Co-ops get paid sick leave, just like full-time employees do. And" - he nodded toward Chris - "your other new dad happens to be a doctor who's more than happy to write you a note saying you need some time off. Maybe just a day or three. It'll all be fine."

Ted's grin lingered, and I felt something in me shift. That smile - steady, warm, and certain - just won the audition for the role of my new dad.

And that was all I could take. I swear I'm not a crybaby, but today would make it hard to prove otherwise. As my tears spilled over again, wetting my baby-bearded cheeks, Chris and Ted double-teamed me with another "dad hug." My second one of the night, and just as overwhelming as the first.

The front door opened, and Corey walked in, stopping mid-step as he caught me tightly wrapped in his fathers' arms. He chuckled, his familiar grin lighting up the room. "I was only gone 20 minutes, and you guys made my puppy cry again, didn't you?"

He motioned to me, his eyes softening. "Come here, my Ollie."

Ted and Chris released me, their arms falling away with a gentle pat on my back, and I walked straight into Corey's embrace. "It's okay, Corey. I swear these are good tears. But, um, yeah, I've gotta stop crying in front of you guys so much. I'm sorry."

Corey's voice was gentle, grounding me as he said, "Once again, Ollie, don't be sorry. But you really need to learn that in 'Texan,' it's 'y'all,' not 'you guys.'"

I smiled, surrounded by three wonderful men, and leaned in to kiss the one closest to me - the one who brought me home to a new family.

CHAPTER 9: BAD PUP, FUN PUP

We said our goodnights and retreated to - wow - *my* new bedroom. Thankfully, it had a queen-sized bed. Also thankfully, we escaped Ted and Chris before they could issue any new warnings about me and Corey exploring "new levels of intimacy." Lurd, I'm beyond grateful their bedroom is on the other side of the house.

The attached bathroom only had a tub shower, so we took turns brushing our teeth and showering. Damn, I couldn't help but admire my beautiful hero through the clear shower curtain. His dark golden fur clung wetly to his bulging muscles. Every movement sent ripples through his flexing form as he soaped himself up. And then there was... *everything else.* His slightly plumped, but still casually flaccid cock and balls, perfectly framed by his dark blond bush, were mesmerizing. I couldn't stop myself from imagining catching the water dripping off its head with my tongue.

Corey noticed my gaze and grinned, his voice tinged with amusement. "Hey, Ollie, so does brushing your teeth always give you a hardon?"

I rinsed my mouth out, trying and failing not to laugh. "Laugh it up," I said, giving him my best hero-worship gaze. Then, with mock innocence, I added, "No, but watching the man I'm about to go to bed with washing his godlike body in the shower sure does."

Before he could reply, I demurely reached between the clear curtain and the tiled wall, turning off his hot water with a quick flick. Corey let out a shocked gasp as the spray went cold, and I darted back into the bedroom, grinning like a kid who'd just pulled off the ultimate prank.

A few minutes later, a barely dry Corey casually strolled into the room with an air of confidence that somehow felt absolutely commanding. I was busy admiring more of his family pictures when his voice cut through my thoughts. "Alright, my *bad* boy - underwear off!"

He plopped his naked, furry butt onto his - er, our - bed with a smirk that was maybe still a little mischievous but mostly stern and demanding. "I want you face down, over my knees young man - now!"

For a second, I wasn't sure how serious he was. Then he broke character just long enough to whisper, "You seemed to like my smacks earlier this morning." His quick smile and wink melted away any hesitation, leaving me grinning like an idiot.

I removed my boxer briefs and freed my hard 7 inches. Corey's stern face returned as he scooted further back on the mattress and patted his lap to indicate where he wanted me to be. I started to utter an apology, but he immediately shushed me and seductively stated, "It's too late for that, boy. You're going to have to take your punishment like a man."

I was already starting to shiver again and I knew I was going to leave a trail of precum extending across Corey's big furry quads. I crawled onto the bed and then pensively moved over Corey's lap. He firmly pushed my butt down as I lowered my torso to my elbows and let my legs straighten out behind me on the bed. My self-lubed erection easily slid down between Coreys legs and I let a moan escape. This is freaking awesome.

"My pup, you've been such a good boy all day, but then you had to go and be bad right before bed. Now you have to suffer the consequences." I felt his right hand gently touch the blond dusting of hairs on my butt cheeks before making full contact. He began rubbing my glutes and making them part just enough that my hole was exposed to the cool room air each time his hand moved from one cheek to the other.

I just barely, and mostly involuntarily, humped into his lap, and I heard a "No-no, not yet baby boy." And his hand left my cheek. Less than a second ticked by before I felt the inevitable slap of his big hand. It stung, it almost hurt, but it mostly just completely blew my mind. Damn! I like being a bad boy! And I let a gasp escape my lips. Corey cupped his left hand over my mouth and cooed me to hush.

I moaned into his palm and didn't have to wait long for my next ass cheek slap. It sent quakes of pleasure through my whole body. This time his hand remained on my butt and he once again massaged my cheeks. Pleasure with a little bit of pain? Yes Sir! Once again, I humped between his legs. Once again, I was rewarded with another slap.

From the back of my overstimulated mind, I heard his soft and lusty voice say, "One more my boy, just to make both cheeks even." And I immediately felt one final exhilarating sting. "Now we can let the fun begin." Corey almost removed his hand from my mouth, but instead, offered his fingers to my lips. "Open up baby boy and get them all nice and covered with spit. Because I think you know what hole they're going into next."

If Corey thought he'd stretched his jock strap beyond its limit, he must have some idea of what he's doing to the boundaries of my sexual experience right now. My mind was exploding as his fingers gently forced their way into my willing mouth. And I readily sucked them in. In and out, fuck, in and out. Corey spoke, "Now that's my good pup, and here's his treat."

I felt his thumb and index finger exposing my hole as he removed his fingers from my mouth and released a perfectly aimed wad of his own spit directly onto my quivering hole. He slowly massaged my sphincter using his spit-wet fingers then finally started applying pressure. I raised my hips up to help him out, and then filled the room with an uncontrollable moan as they slid in to my grateful rectum. For the third time today, Corey was showing me what my bottom was made for.

He gave me my final instructions: "Okay my Ollie, you may start humping my lap now. I'm going to make sure my initial examination of your prostate was correct. Oh, and I might do this again if I feel like you're getting too lost in your inner monologue." Another slap, another wave of ecstasy. I started sliding my leaking dick between Corey's flexing leg muscles. All while he started making my prostate sing the song of its people.

I tried; I swear I tried to make this last. I mean, sure I'm 19, but this would be my third load of the day, so I was hopeful about my stamina. Nope! I made it to ten, maybe fifteen thrusts before I stuttered a "C-C-Corey" and started shooting my cum between his thick thighs. I quivered and shook while my orgasm rolled over me. When I finally started calming down, Corey's fingers slowly left my twitching hole and his hand gently rubbed my reddened cheeks. He leaned over my body and kissed my temple.

"Damn, Ollie," Corey said, his voice low, filled with a mix of amazement and satisfaction. "I totally didn't plan that. But I think we're figuring out that we're pretty darned sexually compatible. Are you okay, buddy?"

I let out a soft laugh, still catching my breath. "Corey, last night, I was sleeping in my Bronco. Now, after yet another amazing experience, I'm about to spend the night in the arms of my Norse God. Every-thing we've done today and tonight has been incred-ible. Yes, sir - I definitely like it when my Corey takes control!" I hesitated, a grin tugging at my lips. "But... I should probably get up before we ruin the comforter."

Corey laughed; a deep, warm sound that made me feel utterly at ease. "My bad. Like I said, totally spon-taneous. But I really don't care about the bedspread. That was absolutely worth it. Damn!"

I finally lifted myself from Corey's lap, thankfully to discover that most of my, um, *contribution*, had ended up trapped in the golden fur of his thighs. The sight made my face flush - until I was hit with the most wicked, obscene thought I'd ever had.

As I got up to my knees, I lowered my face to Corey's lap and licked some of my load out of his fur. And then I kissed him and let him taste my cum. His eyes widened and his tongue dove into my waiting mouth. His intensity grew as he grabbed the back of my head to pull me deeper into our kiss.

When the kiss finally ended, Corey gently said, "Hey now, that's what I had planned for tomorrow's area of exploration. Are you reading ahead?"

I chuckled and got off the bed to get Corey a wet wash rag. "What about you sir? Are you okay for to-night? You're looking pretty stiff there."

"Thank you, but, I'm fine. Besides, I think you'll like where he's going to be spending the night." And I got my last mischievous grin of the day. Corey wiped my mess from his legs and we got the little splatters of my cum off of the bedding.

Corey asked a final question, his voice soft and innocent. "What side of the bed do you want?"

I hesitated, the weight of his simple question hitting me in a way I didn't expect. "I don't know. I've never really slept with anyone before."

"Good point," he said thoughtfully. "How about we just stick with what worked this afternoon? Me on the right, you on the left?"

He turned out the lights, leaving one dim table lamp glowing softly. I appreciated the gesture, the warm light making the room feel even more inviting.

"Great!" I said, my voice bright as my eyes adjusted. I jumped onto the left side and slid under the covers, feeling a mix of excitement and calm. Corey mirrored my movement on the right, and as his front met my back in the middle of the bed, his right arm slipped under my neck and up across my chest, his hand resting over my pecs. His left arm lay gently across my side, his hand tracing slow, soothing circles over my tummy fur.

But the best part was his erection sliding between my cheeks. Fuck. When do we get to explore that level? Corey lazily rubbed his cock over my hole and up my crack just a few times, until it warmly nestled its way into its new home between my cheeks. Then he softly kissed the crown of my head goodnight. I felt so very safe. I almost instantly fell asleep in my champion's embrace.

CHAPTER 10: NIGHTMARE

I've heard that 3:00 a.m. is the perfect time to launch a surprise attack because the victim is usually in their deepest sleep. And I was. But, thank you adrenaline! I woke up with a jolt, instantly ready to fight. *Fuck!* My Bronco is all I have left now. There's no way in hell I'm letting it go. I can't lose everything. I started throwing fists and elbows, my big body doing its best to inflict as much damage as possible.

But I wasn't in a fight with two faceless thugs. I was in the arms of a man who, oh so recently, started caring about me. As the realization hit, I immediately stopped my thrashing, my heart sinking with guilt and dread. *Please, let it at least be past midnight,* I thought. *I can't take crying one more time on the day I just had.*

Corey had somehow dodged my flailing limbs with super hero precision, keeping his composure intact and his arms tightly wrapped around me. In full-blown ER nurse mode, his voice was low and steady, his words trying to find their way into my consciousness through the tangled mess of curls falling over my ear.

"It's okay, Ollie. I've got you. You're in my arms. You're safe, baby boy. You're okay." He kept repeating the words, soothing me until the chaos in my mind began to subside, and lucidity returned. *Lurd, please let me always wake in his arms.*

As soon as I realized where I was, the tears came. I couldn't stop them. "Corey, *I'm sorry*. Please don't let my nightmares ever hurt you. I couldn't handle that. I just couldn't."

"Sssshhh," he whispered, his voice full of quiet strength. "Ollie, it's okay. You've been so close to the end of your rope for so long - you need to understand there's no instant miracle recovery. It's going to take time, even with me, Dad, and Ted reassuring you every day that you're safe now. You *are* safe, my Ollie. You're okay. But, my love, please stop saying you're sorry."

Of all the words my mind just heard, it latched onto one most impossible phrase. "Corey, did you just say *'my love'*?" My sleepy head practically exploded.

"Yes, Ollie. Please don't overthink it. It's just... a sleepy reaction to the situation." He let out a soft laugh, his voice tinged with exhaustion. "Believe me, I've had an emotional day too. But I guess I'll have to tell you sometime about how Dad and Ted got together. Let's just say, I inherited more than just Dad's gay genes." His lips brushed the crown of my head as he asked gently, "Are you okay to go back to sleep?"

I wasn't sure how to feel about everything that had just happened, so I took the simplest route. "Not yet," I mumbled. "I think I need to get some water."

"Can you find your way to the kitchen?" Corey asked, his voice heavy with quickly returning sleep.

My turn to lighten things up. "Lol. Your dads' house is big and beautiful, but I don't think I'll need GPS. Still, I'll take my iPhone - just in case." I gave him a small smile to reassure him. I was really okay, but the thought of slipping back into that nightmare again kept me from just crawling back into bed.

Right as I reached for the bedroom door, Corey's drowsy voice stopped me. "You might wanna put your undies back on first."

Oh. Right. As if I was actually going to walk around my new dads' house stark naked on my first night. Then again... I guess I almost just did. Lurd. I quickly pulled on my boxer-briefs and padded my way down the dimly lit hallway toward the kitchen.

Strangely enough, Ted was already there. In his tighty-whities. For a moment, I silently thanked Corey for the reminder to put on some clothes. *And... well, I guess we really are family now.* Bonus? I had to admit, for a fatherly figure, Ted looked pretty damn good. Big and beefy, with just about as much chestnut fur as Corey had blond. Damn.

"Are you okay, Ollie? What's wrong?" Ted's voice was concerned but steady, a reassuring anchor in the dimly lit kitchen.

"I'm sorry, Ted. I had my customary 3 a.m. nightmare. Only this time, I got to share it with Corey. I think I might've tried to punch him. I didn't even think to warn him before we fell asleep." I paused, trying to compose myself. "Anyway, I just needed to get up and grab some water to clear my head. I swear I'm okay."

Ted's expression softened. "I know you are, Sport - *now*. Come here." He opened his arms, and I stepped into his embrace. My boxer briefs to his just briefs. The moment felt both awkward and strangely comforting.

"Um, is this going on my co-op evaluation report?" I asked, half-joking, half addressing the awkwardness.

Ted chuckled, shaking his head. "Ollie, you need to stop worrying about always being so 'on-point.' You're allowed to just be you." His hand reached up, gently pulling my head down, and he kissed my forehead. Ted wasn't as tall as me, Corey, or Chris, but he was every bit as commanding - and every bit as impressive.

Still fuzzy-headed, I found myself responding with simple sincerity. "I love you too, Dad. Um, where are the glasses? And... why are you up?"

Ted opened a cabinet, pulling down a glass and handing it to me. "Because I'm 52, and I rarely sleep through the night without needing to pee or grab a drink of water myself." His grin was easy, unguarded. "I know you can kind of relate to that now, but I'm glad it was just a nightmare. We can help with that.

And when we do, that'll hopefully make your other problem go away, too."

He gave my shoulder a light squeeze. "Goodnight, Sport. See you in the morning."

I watched my second - wait, first? - new dad shuffle back toward his wing of the house, his presence leaving a lingering sense of calm in the air. I filled my glass with water from the refrigerator and headed quietly back to my room, wondering what damage I might have inflicted on poor Corey.

Thankfully, he was softly snoring when I returned. I sipped from my glass before placing it on the nightstand, the quiet hum of my new home soothed my nerves. Stripping off my boxers, I slipped back into my safe place beside him, doing my best not to disturb his peaceful slumber.

But even in his sleep, Corey instinctively pulled me into his arms, his warmth wrapping around me like a shield. His voice was barely audible, laced with grogginess, as he murmured, "You okay?"

I kissed his hand, letting my lips linger for just a moment before whispering, "I'm fine."

The soft sound of his purring returned, and before long, my own joined his in a peaceful duet, lulling us both into a safe and restful sleep.

CHAPTER 11: OUR FIRST MORNING

Having learned his lesson after waking me from yesterday's nap, Corey's voice floated toward me, warm and inviting - from a safe, non-threatening distance. "Hey, Ollie boy. You slept really well last night - well, except for when you tried to punch me. Time to wake up, my sweet pup."

I yawned and stretched, my body unfurling, greeting the morning in a way it hadn't been able to do in ages. If I'd done this just one morning ago, I would've bashed my knuckles into the Bronco's windows. *Again.* How am I suddenly waking up in this unexpected heaven? My eyes cracked open, and for the first time, I noticed the view from my new bedroom. The backyard and pool gleamed in the bright morning light; the kind of scene that almost felt too good to be real.

Corey caught the moment my eyes adjusted to the daylight, decided it was safe enough to approach, and leaned in to give me a wake-up kiss - completely undeterred by my morning breath. Much to my surprise and delight, he followed it up with a kiss to each of my morning pits. His grin was brighter than the sun-light pouring through the window. "Ollie," he teased, "please never wear deodorant again."

Half-awake, I managed a sleepy chuckle and a squinty-eyed smile, his words leaving me both flustered and amused. But as my mind cleared, one thought rose to the surface - one I couldn't shake. "Corey," I said softly, "did I dream it? Or did you say you loved me last night?"

"I think I maybe did, my boy. But it's right at 9:00 now, and I really want to give you a treat today. Do you mind skipping Starbucks and just chugging down a protein shake?"

"I love a good protein shake. But wait - 9:00? I slept until almost 9:00? I *never* do that. Like, ever."

Corey held up a single finger with the same mock-stern face he gave his dads last night. "Wait - stop! Do *not* say you're sorry. You *needed* it, and I'm pretty sure Dad's right. You need a lot more."

"Fine," I said, conceding with a small smile. "But, um... did I also really try to fight you last night?" My gaze drifted to the water glass on the nightstand, the memory of waking up foggy but lingering.

"It's okay, buddy. We've got a journey ahead of us, and it's how all great stories start. The important part is I'm still going to be here tonight, tomorrow night, and, hopefully, far beyond that."

I leaned up and kissed my sweet Norse God, my chest swelling at the reassurance in his words. "Okay,"

I said, grinning. "What's the plan, my man?"

"Well, good news: you won't need a shower." His smirk turned slightly mischievous. "Bad news: I might be pushing your boundaries again. You do understand that you're beautiful and have an absolutely stunning body, right?"

I stared at him, refusing to nod but secretly appreciating his insistence.

He continued, his tone light but serious. "Do you like cycling?"

My face instantly brightened. "I absolutely love it! It's my favorite off-season way to do 'leg day' without really doing 'leg day.' But my bike and gear are back in Michigan... probably never to be seen again. What did you have in mind?"

Corey's grin widened. "Well, I'm sure you didn't notice it yesterday evening, but there's a bike trail right out in front of the house. It runs through the park along the creek - it's our neighborhood's feeder trail to the Trinity Trails system. That system stretches for miles and miles along the Trinity River. I figured I could introduce you to one of my favorite things."

"That's awesome," I said, already imagining it. "But, like I said, I don't have a bike or gear and... frak, it's 9:00, right? I need to call Jason at LA Fitness and explain my new living situation."

"It's all okay, Ollie." Corey's voice was calm, reassuring. "You can call Jason; I'll shake up the protein, and it'll all work out." He paused, looking me over with a playful glint in his eye. "What's your waist size?"

"Um, 32?"

"Perfect. I'm 34, and biking bibs aren't that exact. I brought two pairs from my house last night - one for you, one for me. Bonus, Dad's bike should almost be exactly your size. So! You'll have Dad's bike and my bibs. All you need to supply is a T-shirt or tank top. Oh... And hint: tank top."

"But what about cleats? I seriously doubt your dad's shoes are exactly my size."

Corey's smirk was already forming. "Still no worries. Dad's pedals are bi - just like he tried to be with my mom that one time." He flashed his first full smirk of the day, clearly proud of his joke. "Cleat clips on one side, flat pedals on the other. All you need are your gym shoes."

I rolled my eyes, but couldn't help smiling. "Is there anything you're not in control of?"

"Many things, Ollie, but I'm doing my best for you." He paused, his smirk softening into something much sweeter. "Now, don't you dare wash those morning pits of yours. Just put your undies on and let's go get that shake. Oh, and by the way - we're a morning underwear family, and I hear you've already seen Ted in his. It's all good."

How does he even remember things I tell him in his sleep? Oh wait - I didn't. I guess Ted did, and that means I'm the last one up. I sighed, pulling my boxer briefs on and picking up my iPhone as Corey's perfectly filled tighty-whities disappeared down the hall.

"I'll be right there," I called after him, dialing my suddenly former second boss. Jason sounded sad to lose my help but happy to gain me as a customer - and even happier about my new living conditions. I guess everyone kinda suspected I was homeless. Dang.

CHAPTER 12: MEET THE DADS

I walked into a much brighter kitchen than the one I'd wandered through last night, and sure enough, there were Chris and Ted, sipping their coffee in nothing but their briefs, sitting at the breakfast nook table. I guess if I want to fit in - and I do - I'll have to switch to tighty-whities soon myself. I only started wearing boxers because my dad told me it'd be a good idea once I'd finally turned into a "big boy."

As soon as I stepped in, they both raised their mugs in unison and wished me a good morning, their voices warm and welcoming. Please, Lurd, let me and Corey look that good in 25 years. No, scratch that - just give me 25 years with my champion and his dads. That's all I ask.

Corey appeared beside me, handed me a mug, and filled it with steaming, freshly brewed coffee. I added a generous amount of sugar, and he grinned. "I knew you were a sweet boy as soon as I saw you," he teased, his tone full of affection.

I blushed, but still managed to walk over and give

each of my new dads a side hug. I'm usually a full-body hug kind of guy, but even after yesterday, there was still something surreal about casually greeting people - who until yesterday - I only knew as my doctor and my mentor. All while they were mostly naked, just starting their Saturday morning routine. It was equal parts awkward and somehow comforting - and strangely, it all just felt like home.

As if on cue, both of them gave me a once-over in an appraising, fatherly way, but it was Ted - who knows me best - who decided to fire the first embarrassing dad comment of the morning. "Damn, Sport! You really are a super co-op!"

Corey walked over, bro-punched him in the arm, and wrapped his bare upper body around mine. "Yes, he is, and I found him first, so he's mine."

Chris looked up from his coffee, chuckle-clearing his throat in that way only an all-knowing dad can. "Actually, he found Ted first, just over three months ago. Then he met me. We just had enough restraint to let him stay fully clothed - until *you* stepped in." Wait, wait. Did my Corey just get double-smirked by both our dads? This is awesome. And, much to my dismay, I giggled. *Again.*

Corey's smile at me was warm, but his tone was mock-scolding once again. "Like you said last night - laugh it up buddy. I'll lose you on the bike trails today."

I put on my best hurt puppy expression and delivered my most pathetic, "But you keep saying you don't want to lose me."

Corey groaned, shaking his head with a big, thoughtful smile. "Damn, I keep forgetting how fast you adapt." Then he turned to Chris. "Oh, hey, Dad, can Ollie borrow your bike for the day? I want to show him at least a little bit of the Trinity Trails. And..." He glanced at me with a smirk that made my skin tingle, "I really want to see him in my cycling bibs."

He leaned down and gave me another morning kiss. It was absolutely perfect - until I remembered I was standing there drinking coffee in just my skin-tight underwear, right in front of our dads.

Chris was this moment's proud recipient of the award for Most Inappropriate Dad Comment. "Well, I'm starting to see that Ollie really could be my son. Corey, maybe you should take care of that before you take him out into the neighborhood in cycling bibs."

In unison, the dads clinked their coffee mugs together, like they'd just delivered the perfect punchline. Somehow, I didn't die of embarrassment - though it felt like I should've. Instead, I surprised myself by going bold. "He seems to know how to do that really well, sirs. But... I'm still not sure about wearing biking shorts in public. I was just expecting gym shorts."

Corey, kind of, sort of, well, at least *ish* came to my rescue. "Ollie, you'll make all the other bikers gawk, lose focus, and ride off the trail. Like I said yesterday - turn around and be proud." He cupped my butt cheek and added, "Well Dads, I guess we're suddenly finishing our coffee back in our room. This is all your fault. I was going to save my next surprise for Ollie until tonight, but now I have to give it to him before we leave. Anyway... so, can Ollie use your bike?"

Chris, completely unfazed, replied drolly, "Sorry, something *big* distracted me." He added an expert dad-joke-pause-for-effect before finishing. "Absolutely, Ollie! Again, son, just take care of that thing before leaving the house." He gave me what I now recognized as the signature Chris-Corey father-son smirk. "And don't forget to shut your door."

Ted immediately chimed in. "Oh God, yes, please. Shut your door, Corey!"

CHAPTER 13: SHUT YOUR DOOR, COREY

As soon as we got to our room, I innocently asked, "What's all that about shutting your bedroom door?"

"It's something they'll never let me live down." His eyes rolling with slight exasperation over the memory, "So, I was 9 when they got together. Over the years, I got very used to seeing my two dads being very affectionate with each other. I loved it, it made me happy. Plus, since we have a private pool, speedo cut trunks became the norm, still are. And several times, I accidently caught them both in the pool or hot tub naked. It never bothered me and no one ever made any big deal about anyone's level, *or lack*, of clothing. It just didn't matter.

He looked into my eyes, bring me into his tale, "I was the exact opposite of you, at least according to what you told me about your journey through puberty. I was the *first* kid in my class to get pubes and a *big boy dick*. Unlike you, I didn't handle my situation as well."

He glanced away, flashing a bit of some long-ago embarrassment, "I always felt like everyone was looking at me and whispering about my big hairy dick. It really started to upset me. I came home after a particularly bad day of junior high school and, well, dad *is* a urologist. So, I stormed in, found him, dropped my pants and demanded to know if I was normal."

My eyes were large as saucers, wondering how my father would have reacted. Corey regained his smile and continued, "After he got over the shock of my brashness, he chuckled - in a fatherly way - and told me that I was very much *above* normal. He assured me that I was probably just a few months ahead of the other boys in my class and that they would soon catch up with me and lose interest.

Corey was apparently just getting to the heart of the story, "Because I'd breached the subject and, well, was still standing there with my dick hanging out, he asked if I'd had a wet dream yet. Then he had to explain what that was. He also explained about masturbation and how it was 'perfectly normal' for me to start doing it. But only in my room.

"I didn't have to be told twice. I picked up my pants and undies and ran to my room. I was hard before I made it past the kitchen. I jumped on my bed and I think it took maybe 45 seconds before I experienced my first orgasm and shot my first load all over my chest and stomach." Corey tried not to chuckle at my shocked expression, "But wait pup, there's more...

And what did I immediately do next? I yelled for Dad and Ted to come to my room. 'Dads! You're not gonna believe what I just did!'"

My jaw was once again on the floor as Corey gleefully reached er, the *climax* of his story, "Imagine their surprise when they walked in to find their totally naked son, drenched in his own cum, his hand still around his hard dick, proudly presenting his accomplishment. 'Guys, this is awesome! Is it okay to do this as much as I want?'

"After they stopped laughing, they assured me that yes, 'jacking off' is every teenage boy's favorite hobby. Then, in unison, they added, 'But maybe shut your door before you do it next time.' Unfortunately, I kept forgetting that part and they kept walking by my room right at the wrong time, well, because there were *a lot* of wrong times. 'Shut your door, Corey!' became our house's most overused catch phrase."

My mouth was still agape as I heard him seductively say, "So, Ollie, shut the door."

CHAPTER 14: SOLVING A HARD PROBLEM

Corey easily slipped back into his nurse command mode, his demeanor that starts sending shivers all through my body. "Drop those boxer-briefs my boy, time to make that protein shake."

Still frazzled by his story, my inner monologue was all, *Wait? what?!* But I dropped my drawers as I was told, and freed my now very hard dick. Corey dropped his briefs as well and moved in to give me a long and sensual kiss. When he came up for air, he gently pushed me back onto our bed. And slowly leaned forward, arms on the bed on either side of me, crawling toward my torso, forcing me to lie back, while giving me one more quick kiss.

This time I absolutely understood that I was his prey. I shivered as his lips and breath made their now almost familiar way back down my body. This time, he didn't stop at my belly button. He took a deep breath of my pubes, and then ever so gently placed his lips on the exposed head of my very attentive cock.

But then raised up, "Ollie, I rarely get to suck an uncircumcised cock, just stop me if I do anything wrong." Then he tenderly took my exposed head into his mouth and slowly started twirling his tongue under what little loose foreskin remained around the top of my shaft.

"Damn! You're not doing anything wrong! Is it supposed to feel this amazing?"

Corey gave me an evil, lusty smile, and proceeded to worship my throbbing, leaking dick with his tongue. He let a proud appraisal slip out: "Ollie, your precum tastes amazing. Pure and sweet, exactly like you." I smiled between gasps of new and unexpected waves of pleasure.

He then started taking more and more of my shaft into his mouth. While his tongue kept dancing around everything it could reach. His fist was wrapped around the lower inches of my shaft as he started an up and down motion that I'd seen in so many pornos, I just had no clue how amazing the real deal felt. My balls inevitably started rising into firing position. Corey noticed it as well.

He let my over stimulated cock slide from his mouth. "Not yet pup, here's a preview of what's in store for tonight." He moved his face lower, and for the second time, I felt his tongue on my balls. He attentively bathed each one, then lifted them up and continued south. I felt his magical, wide tongue on my shaved-smooth taint, and I had to fight back a way too loud moan. It was as if his tongue was licking the whole of my body.

"I knew you were going to like that." He smiled, "Just wait until I go lower tonight."

I almost comprehended what his innuendo was telling me, but I just couldn't believe it, so I simply responded with my standard, "Y-yes sir!" He returned his attention to my dripping dick and it only took a few more minutes of licks with his tongue and strokes with his fist before I was delivering my protein into his hungry mouth. I saw stars and comets and whole galaxies before my senses returned to normal.

As I was trying to calm down, Corey had crawled up the bed and was again by my side, gently rubbing my furry tummy and kissing my neck. I eventually uttered, "May I return the favor? My Norse God."

He smiled and replied, "Hey, you need some protein too. However, you won't believe this, but I'm much better at giving blow jobs than I am at receiving them. I know that sounds stupid. I mean, they feel great, but I might need to take control to cross the finish line. Is that okay?"

I was like, you *prefer doing* what you just did to me? And this is a problem? But instead, I simply said, "I'd love to try my best sir."

"I know you will, Ollie. I'm not sure you've noticed this yet, but I really like being a little dominant in our fun. And I think you like being a bit submissive. Am I right?"

Fuck, I'd honestly never realized that before, but, well, fuck. "Yes, sir!"

"Good boy! Now, off the bed and on your knees." Corey got up from the bed as well.

I immediately complied and suddenly Corey's cock was throbbing right in front of my face. And like Corey, my first instinct was to grab his erection, move it aside and inhale the scent of his pubes followed by his balls. I knew I'd love his scent, and I wasn't wrong. I couldn't stop myself from moving lower where his scent intensified. But I didn't lick anything like he did; I wasn't sure I was ready to do that, so I returned to his pubes.

He cupped his hand under my chin and looked deeply into my eyes. "Why don't you start off just doing what comes naturally, and we can go from there." I took that as my cue and I again took his massive member in my fist but this time I maneuvered the shaft to point down in my direction. I tentatively licked the precum that was about to drip from his slit and immediately realized it was the taste I never knew I needed to have on my tongue.

From that moment on, I knew exactly what to do, I was just so shocked at how badly I *needed* to do it. I couldn't get enough of Corey's cock. I loved his taste and his primal scent. I kept trying to take as much of his shaft in my mouth as I could. But I'd always wind up choking after the first 4 inches or so. So, I tried another approach and simply licked and slid my lips and tongue all the way up and down the bottom side of his pole. I was having the time of my life, all the while looking up at Corey to make sure he was enjoying it. I think he was. At least, I loved the smile he was giving me.

"Damn Ollie! Aren't you the eager pup? I can't believe this is your first time, but then again, I also keep forgetting how fast you adapt to new situations. With a lot of *practice*," he gave me a wink, "you'll be a pro and be able to take me a lot deeper. But for right now, may I suggest an alternative way to get me over the edge?"

I didn't want to release his manhood from my lips yet, so I simply nodded.

"Okay, pup spit on your palm and firmly wrap it around my shaft. Use it as a buffer to keep me from going too deep into your mouth."

I immediately understood what Corey was asking. And I let him take over. He started slowly thrusting his cock through my fist and into my mouth. I just concentrated on keeping my teeth safely out of the way, my tongue on his frenulum, and enjoying how amazing it felt to be getting Corey so excited.

He placed his right hand under my chin again and his left on my cheek. "You look so incredibly hot right now my beautiful pup, I'm really close. Are you okay to swallow my load?" I gave him a *genuine* hero worshiping look and another nod. He gave me the biggest smile that was all too quickly replaced with his very manly 'O' face. My mouth was soon filled with shot after shot of his protein. I reflexively swallowed all I could, but I knew some of it was dripping out of the corners of my mouth.

After his shivers and quakes subsided, my dominant Corey slowly left to be replaced by my protector Corey. I felt absolutely safe with both. He immediately asked, "Are you okay? That was incredible. I can't believe you did so well for your first time. You are my very good pup." I stood up and kissed him. He licked up the parts of his load I couldn't swallow and we shared it in our continued kiss.

"Are you safe to get into our cycling bibs now?" Corey teased.

"Absolutely - for at least fifteen minutes. But once I see you in yours, I might throw wood again." I grinned sheepishly. "Also, um... you do realize that little fun talk we had with the dads kinda derailed our quest for real protein shakes, right?"

Corey chuckled, his mischievous grin lighting up the room. "You don't miss a thing. Put your bibs on, and let's finally - *really, really-really* - go get our shakes."

****

Corey's bibs fit me perfectly, and I almost felt like one of my wrestler friends from high school - except for the sewn-in seat padding. Wrestler singlets definitely don't have that. The padding made it feel like someone was cupping my butt crack. But hey, since meeting Corey, that's become one of my new favorite feelings. I decided to put a thin tank top over the bibs, just like Corey suggested.

Corey gave me an appraising look, his eyes scanning me from head to toe. "Dayam," he simply said. I took that as a "good to go."

I shot the same look right back at him. His bibs accentuated his muscles and all of his bulges perfectly. "You know, looking at you is going to keep me, well, *enthusiastic* for the whole ride, right?"

Corey grinned, his tone dripping with playful confidence. "Hey, that just means more fun when we're done."

We finally had our real shakes, topped our tires off with a few pumps of air, donned our helmets, bid our dads goodbye, and finally started our ride. Chris' bike really did fit me perfectly, but I missed being clipped in. Still, I was being given the chance to ride again and I was happy.

CHAPTER 15: ON THE PATH TOGETHER

We rode north along the trail as it wound through my beautiful new neighborhood until we made a sharp left turn and ducked under Hulen Street. After a few more quick turns and a street crossing, we were suddenly overlooking the Trinity River - or maybe the Trinity Creek? The trail continued over the river at a low-water crossing. I swear, the Trinity couldn't be more than two or three feet deep, but it was still pretty, just different from the bigger rivers I was used to.

Corey stopped before we started the descent to the riverbed. "See that exposed bedrock there where our little creek empties into the river? When I was a kid, you could find ammonite fossils there. But they were soft, like moist clay. I took a few home and did what any kid would do - I baked them in the oven to harden them into stone."

He grimaced dramatically, and I could already tell

where the story was headed. "The dads weren't too happy to find their oven full of stinking, hot river mud. And, sadly, my experiment didn't really work anyway. But I still say I should've gotten credit for being so creative. Nope! Instead, I got grounded."

I laughed, imagining a young, *earnestly* mischievous Corey, and found myself wishing I'd known him back then. "That's hilarious. You definitely deserved points for creativity."

Corey grinned. "Okay, the left - or west - trail will take us out to Lake Benbrook. It's gorgeous out there. But I think we should head right, or east, into Trinity Park and then past downtown. Ready to really roll?"

I nodded eagerly. "Let's do it."

Corey coasted down the slope, crossing the low-water dam before pedaling up the other bank, with me close behind. Once we reached the main trail, it widened enough for us to ride side by side. We only had to slip back into tandem when someone was coming toward us. Our ride alternated between relaxed conversation and competitive bursts of speed, racing each other for dominance. I'd say I was at a disadvantage because I couldn't clip in, but honestly, I was having the most fun I've had in forever. This was an amazing city perk I never even knew existed.

When we reached the heart of Trinity Park, Corey signaled for us to exit the trail. He led us to a shady picnic table by a much-needed water fountain. As Corey leaned in for a big drink, I couldn't resist speaking up. "I wondered why we didn't bring any water bottles."

"Um, normally I do, but..." Corey glanced at me with a sheepish grin. "You in those bibs got me all flustered and I forgot. Thankfully, this part of the trail has a few water fountains. What's my 'bad' count up to now?"

"Zero! You're perfect." My reply earned me a hug and a quick kiss. I grinned, adding, "Careful, though - the dads won't be happy if I accidentally shock anyone in the park."

Corey chuckled and pointed toward a food truck parked nearby. "Wanna take a break and gaze at the skyline? Maybe grab a light lunch while we're at it?"

I thought it was a great idea - *both* of my protein shakes were long gone. As we walked toward the food truck to check out the menu, I glanced back at the skyline. "The view is really cool from here," I said, then hesitated for a second before adding, "but there's something I've been meaning to ask you. It's about something you called me yesterday... and something you and the dads keep calling me now."

Corey raised an eyebrow, intrigued. I pressed on. "So, right before you, uh, shaved my taint, and again before we napped, you called me 'Ollie Otter.' And you keep calling me 'pup,' which I love, but... do they mean anything beyond just being *pet* names?"

He gave me a dramatic wince at my terrible pun, but his face quickly lit up. "Ooh! Time for the well-*prac-*

ticed gay to educate his baby gay again!"

I laughed, shaking my head. "My cousin would so kill me. Yes please - teach me, sir!"

By the time we reached the front of the line, we'd both decided on a couple of ridiculously delicious-looking hotdogs - *apiece* - and a couple bottles of Powerade. Both were perfect for quenching my hunger and thirst. I couldn't wait to hear his answer as we carried our lunch over to a shady spot overlooking the river and skyline beyond.

After we wolfed down our first hotdog, Corey began his explanation. "Alright, Ollie, first off, I just like thinking of you as my cute little puppy. But also, a lot of gays refer to their body types - or even personality types - as animals. For example, Ted is almost a muscle bear. He's bulky and furry, but not quite big enough to be a classic bear. Bears are usually hairy, hunky-chunky guys known for being friendly and huggable. There are also 'cubs,' who are either younger bears or guys who prefer being a bit more submissive.

"Then we've got otters - furry, wiry guys, who are thinner instead of bulky. Honestly, I was just trying to be clever when I called you an otter - mostly just trying to keep you engaged. Because, with your muscles... Well, they're way too big for you to be a true otter. Unless that's what you want to be, of course. A lot of all this comes down to *your* preference. Personally, I think you're more of a college jock right now. I mean, sure, I could shave you down, make the rest of you match your smooth taint, and call you a 'twunk'

- a muscled-up twink - but that would never fit you. And honestly, I'd never want to do that."

He paused just long enough to flash me a smirk. "If I had to choose my own animal designation, I'd probably go with 'wolf.' Furry, muscled, and, as you've discovered, a little dominant - at least in bed." His smirk deepened, sending my heart racing. "Dad's pretty close to being the same, though he claims he doesn't do labels. He just prefers to call himself a 'muscle dad.' So, Ollie, since I'm a wolf and you're my boy, I like calling you my pup. Actually, I love thinking of you as my beautiful wolf pup. Is that okay?"

I was practically melting, loving every single word coming out of his mouth. Did he even need to ask? Grinning, I replied, "I have a wolf for protection. I'm the happiest pup on the planet."

Public or not, I couldn't resist. I leaned in and kissed *my wolf*, feeling completely at home in his arms.

CHAPTER 16: SUMMIT DECLARATIONS

After our "gay zoo" talk over lunch, we continued along the Trinity Trail toward downtown Fort Worth. At this point the trail was a ribbon of concrete sandwiched between the river on our right and a tall levee on our left. It was obvious we were deep in the Trinity's floodplain. As we got closer to the skyline, I realized we were approaching the bridge we'd driven over the night before on our way to Joe T's. What I hadn't noticed in the dark was that another branch of the Trinity merged with the river just before the bridge.

Instead of taking the bike bridge to follow the combined river east, Corey veered sharply left, following the northbound branch of the river. After a short ride north, we stopped in front of a tall, rectangular concrete monolith jutting up from the floodplain. The structure was stark and imposing, completely out of place against the natural backdrop. I was intrigued. Corey leaned his Trek gently on the grass, and I followed suit.

"Ollie," he began, with a sheepish, almost shy, grin spreading across his face. "This is totally silly and a huge indulgence for me, but ever since I was a junior in high school and my best friend did this with his girlfriend - and I was crushed, because, well, I had a crush on him - I've been wanting to do this with someone special. Will you follow me up?"

He motioned me around to the far side of the structure, where steel bar 'n's were embedded in the concrete, forming a ladder all the way to the 20-foot summit. Without hesitation, Corey boldly grabbed the rungs and began climbing. He glanced back at me with a now hopeful smile. Right on cue, my good-boy brain vigilantly whispered: *This probably isn't allowed.* But Corey's expression erased the thought entirely, and I followed him up.

As I crested the concrete summit, it was both awe-inspiring and, I'll admit, a little anticlimactic at the top. Turns out, it was just an over-glorified storm sewer manhole cover, raised this high to avoid flooding. Still, it offered a stunning, unobstructed view of Fort Worth's skyline. Picture perfect. As soon as I stood beside Corey, he pulled me into his arms and kissed me with a passion that made my head spin. Then, he tipped his head back and, honest to god, howled. It was deep and primal, and I couldn't help but smile with amazement. Note to self: I definitely need to learn how to do that.

But Corey wasn't finished. He turned to face the

skyscrapers and stood fast. He took a deep breath then bellowed, at full volume: "I've met the pup of my dreams, Oliver Aaron Carson! I want him to always be mine!" As his voice leapt into the open sky, two passing bikers looked up, laughing as they both gave us a thumbs up. Corey doubled over, laughing himself. "That seemed way more romantic when I was 17."

I smiled, absolutely feeling the sincerity of his declaration. Hey, I was still a teenager for a few more months, and I thought it was incredibly sweet. Without overthinking it, I added my own proclamation: "My Norse God, Corey Rainer, rescued me and gave me a new family! I'm proud to be his pup!" My voice carried over the quiet of the park, and we both dissolved into laughter, standing atop a storm drain and shouting our new love truths to the world.

Naturally, we had to take a few selfies to mark the occasion. Corey's arm pulled me close as we posed, the city skyline behind us. Of course, at least one shot had to include us kissing. And, well, we might have kissed a little too long for public decency. Oops. I guess I'm still on track to shock a few park-goers today - my bad.

As our selfie kisses ended, a thought struck me. "Um, Corey, I promise not to use it against you anytime soon, but I don't know your middle name. What is it?"

His smile turned mischievous. "It's so close to yours, I'm Corey Allan. And if I ever make you mad during an argument, you have every right to use it." We laughed, and of course, we kissed one last time before starting the climb down.

I'd never thought of myself as being afraid of heights, but stepping back over the edge to descend was definitely scarier than the climb up. My heart was still pounding a bit by the time I was just three rungs from the ground. That's when Corey grinned and said, "Trust fall! Let go."

I hesitated, glancing down at him. My head was only about three feet above his, so with a leap of faith, I released the rung and let myself fall backward. He caught me effortlessly, his strong arms wrapping around me like a safety net.

"Corey, you know I weigh 170, and I want to get bigger, right? We might not be able to do this much longer."

"Hey, I'm 225, and I'm pretty sure I'll be able to catch you for decades to come." His confidence, as always, felt unshakable. I got another kiss for good measure, and I couldn't help but silently hope for those decades too.

After readjusting my still present, er, *enthusiasm* to point discreetly under my tank, we continued our ride north before eventually turning back at a major road. We retraced our path through downtown and back into Trinity Park, the scenery just as gorgeous in reverse. As we crossed under I-30 and began paralleling University Drive again, something caught my eye that I'd completely missed earlier.

"Corey, what's that miniature train bridge for?"

He grinned, clearly pleased by my curiosity. "It's for a kid's train ride that goes from the zoo, over the river, into the park, and then loops back. I used to ride it all the time when I was in grade school. It shut down for several years, but they recently reopened it. Now the cool trend is for people my age to ride it and re-live their childhood memories."

"You know we have to do that soon, right?"

Corey nodded with a playful glint in his eye. "Absolutely!"

CHAPTER 17: FOREST PLAY PLACE

We retraced our path over the low water crossing and headed back into our neighborhood. Even though I was still learning the lay of the land, I was pretty sure we'd just passed our house. But I kept following my Norse God - wait! Now my wolf.

After about a mile, the trail veered away from the boulevard and disappeared into what looked like a forest. I blinked, trying to make sense of it. I mean, we're still surrounded by an established neighborhood, right? There's no way there can just suddenly be a forest. As I was coaxing my brain to explain things, Corey signaled for us to pull off the trail, right where the trees seemed thickest.

Corey dismounted and stood beside his bike. "Walk your bike and follow me." I didn't question it - I just obeyed.

There was a nearly hidden trail winding between the trees, almost like it had been designed to stay secret. The further in we went, the more the world outside faded away. Finally, we emerged into what felt like a room formed entirely by the dense thicket. The greenery wove together to create walls, almost like nature had conspired to hide this magical place.

"This is totally an optical illusion," Corey explained, his voice low and reverent. "It only works in the spring and summer. There are houses just above and behind us, but it feels private right now." He leaned his bike against a big tree that framed one side of the "room's" entrance. I mirrored him, placing my bike against its twin on the left.

Corey turned and lifted his arms, offering me an embrace. Without hesitation, I moved into him, nestling myself into his right side - nuzzling closer to his pit. He must have immediately sensed what I wanted because he smiled and raised his arm, granting my silent wish.

Oh my lurd. Fresh, clean, Corey biking sweat. This had to be exactly what he meant by that "post-workout bliss" scent he mentioned yesterday. I reveled in it, letting the world fall away as his musk filled my senses. My beard caught the scent, and for the first time, I understood completely - yes, this is exactly what beards are for.

He raised my head for a kiss from his pup - one who now carried his scent. And I'm not sure how, but this kiss felt like a brand-new first kiss, without erasing the magic of the ones Corey had already given me. It clearly meant a lot to Corey too.

"Okay, pup," he said softly, his voice a mix of playfulness and seriousness, "I'm never going to ask you to do anything you aren't ready for, but if I promise we're totally safe here, would you be up for a little exploratory fun?"

I couldn't help but tease him. "There isn't anything you're accidentally forgetting to tell me about, is there? No more surprises like, 'Oops, that's what a catheter moving through your prostate feels like'?" I attempted my best smirk, even as my cheeks betrayed me with a blush.

He chuckled, his grin both apologetic and mischievous. "I swear, no surprises this time. This is all fun, I promise." Then he leaned in, his eyes locking with mine in that way that makes me feel both exposed and completely safe. "Now, arms up, my pup. Trust me."

I did. He immediately lifted my tank top over my head while still taking the time to bask in my sweaty pits. "Remember, I grew up here, I know we're safe." I shot him a quizzical look as he pushed my bib straps off of my shoulders and seductively started pulling them down past my thighs. I was exposed to the world. My quizzical look flashed into a look of concern. Corey cupped my cheek and said "I've got you pup." There's no way I can't believe him, but he's pushing it.

He wrapped his hand around my exposed cock and started our kiss. Both our beards had the scent of the other and I was suddenly dizzy and even more hard in Corey's fist. He stopped to step back as he pulled his tank off over his head and lowered his bibs down as far as mine. He was already hard as well.

We resumed our embrace. Me slowly jacking his leaking cock, him mirroring the same to mine. This might be a little exposed for me, but it's taking our fun up to yet another level.

Lol, he can obviously still read my mind because he immediately said, "I have a new level we can try. I know you're not ready for the whole *big event* yet, but there's something we can do that's not quite *practicing*, but still feels really good for both of us. Trust me?" His face presenting an earnest and excited but still encouraging smile.

The man has me naked in a forest, in the middle of a city neighborhood, with my once again overly earnest cock drooling in his hand, and he's asking me to trust him even more? Lurd. But, he's my wolf. I nodded my head.

"Okay Ollie pup, turn around, put your hands on the big tree behind you, and lean forward. I promise, we are not 'practicing,' we're maybe just 'practicing for practicing.'" And I got a big sweet Corey smile. I think I know where this is going and I think I'm going to like it.

I turned around and leaned into the tree, exposing my playing field to Corey. I felt him move in closer behind me and then I heard him spit and I felt his wet fingers rub my hole and move up. I felt another glob of spit hit and run down my crack. And then Corey solidified his stance and allowed his throbbing cock to return to last night's sleeping place. Only his cock wasn't sleepy right now. He leaned his chest over my back and kissed my neck, right behind my ear. Damn! There's another new level!

My slick playing field was loving its new play mate. "Are you ready pup?" I was already doing my now familiar uncontrollable quivering. Corey took that as a 'yes.' He gave me a very sexy growl and playfully nipped my earlobe.

He moved his right arm across my pec, with his hand almost at my neck. His left hand softly landed on my lower abs and then immediately moved south into my blond thicket until it reached my tree. And as he started stroking my cock, he also slowly started humping his across my twitching hole and up my crack.

He whispered in my ear. "You have three jobs my boy. I'm going to start putting more of my weight on you, so please don't let us fall into the tree." I nodded. "And you can arch your back and start pushing against me as I thrust between your cheeks. Most importantly, Ollie, just relax and enjoy our new level." He finished his instructions by moving his hand to my throat and nudging my jaw to turn into his for a kiss. Dayam.

He kept slowly humping my crack and I quickly matched his rhythm and pushed back as instructed. Every time his pole slid over my hole I let out a moan. And those moans pushed my wolf to higher levels of excitement. Only to then be matched by mine. After several euphoric minutes of us climbing ever higher on our new ladder together, we both knew we were approaching the summit.

Our rate hit its maximum speed. His sweaty, furry chest was plastered against my sweaty smooth back. His arms were holding his prey/mate in place. As his hips were furiously humping me like the beast he was. His beard was entangling itself with mine as his face forcefully nudged its way against my cheek over my shoulder. We were both too gone to maintain our kiss. This was a whole new mind-blowing level. I arched my back even more, begging him to keep going.

Between his gritted teeth, Corey growled, "That's right pup, you're only reacting the way your body is telling you to." Nothing this raw and intense can last for long. It was mere moments before I felt his hot seed splatter all over my back. And it was only a few dizzying seconds later when mine shot all over my supporting tree's trunk.

Corey started kissing my cheek as his embrace returned to a less rib cracking level. "Are you okay Ollie? That got a bit intense."

"Fuck, Corey, er, sorry, frak! I loved every second of that! Damn! My wolf! That was pure euphoria. And well, I think my new favorite tree might get pregnant."

Much to my delight, Corey smacked my cheeks again and laughed softly. "If that were possible, this little clearing would probably be the world's busiest maternity ward by now. Not that Dad and Ted would've cared, but back when my classmates started catching up with me in the puberty department, this was my favorite spot to bring them. It just seemed way more forbidden and naughty here than in my bedroom."

I raised an eyebrow, only half-teasing. I wasn't absolutely onboard with Corey admitting he was his classmates' sexual awakening cruise director. "So, what - you waited for your friends to sprout their first pubes, then gave them a private invitation to your enchanted forest hideaway?"

"Pup! That's not what I meant." Corey looked genuinely amused. "I wasn't recruiting! I was just always the guy my friends could talk to when they had questions, or needed advice, or - well - when they were freaking out about things they couldn't talk to anyone else about. I guess I've always been a protector at heart, even back then. And yeah, maybe that meant sharing some no-judgment, no-pressure moments of adolescent discovery.

In case you didn't get it from 'Shut your door, Corey,' I've always had a really positive, fun attitude about jacking off. It was nothing to ever be ashamed of. And believe me, it was never anything more serious than some mutual curiosity and a little harmless fun. But hey, that tree has seen a lot of teenage… well, let's just say *history*. I guarantee you, though, it's never been happier than you made it today."

Corey's honesty, as always, left me grinning. He had

a way of making even the most awkward revelations seem perfectly normal. He had pulled his redemption off like the shining champion I was hoping he really was. I reached for his hand, silently letting him know I wasn't judging. He accepted my implied apology.

We laughed softly as we adjusted our bibs and slipped back into our tank tops, doing our best to look respectable - or at least as respectable as two guys in cycling shorts could be. Floating from our moment together, the ride back seemed to fly by. Before I knew it, we were coasting up to the front door, my heart still soaring from everything that had just happened in Corey's secret world.

CHAPTER 18: BUSTED

Ted was in the kitchen as we walked through to our bedroom. Before we could even say, "Hey, Ted," he gave us a fatherly look that clearly said, *You two know you aren't getting away with any of this.* Then, turning specifically to Corey, he said with a perfect calmness, "I saw you two ride past the house about 45 minutes ago." His gaze shifted to me. "I'm guessing Corey showed you his favorite forest play place?" Then back to Corey, "If my favorite co-op student is walking funny, you're grounded, young man."

Corey chuckled, effortlessly dodging the accusation. "Hey, that's not fair! He's already walking funny because I had to shave his furry butt crack yesterday morning. Besides, we just had good, clean fun. My new pup inspired me to relive my high school days today. It's been awesome."

Ted rolled his eyes with the perfect blend of exasperation and affection. "Just please tell me he didn't howl."

The moment my face betrayed me, Ted immediately added, "You're grounded, Corey." His chuckle was like the cherry on top.

I jumped in to defend my champion. "But I swear, it was downtown on a weirdly tall storm sewer and not in the woods."

Ted's grin widened as he looked back at me. "Let me guess - you also now know how long he's been waiting to stand up there with someone?" I nodded, feeling the warmth of his hand on my back before he sent us on our way.

As we headed to our room, Ted called after us, "Chris should be back from the store in about 30 minutes. We've got reservations at Celebrations for 6:30. We figured that'd be another fun restaurant to introduce Ollie to. Now, go get cleaned up. You both smell like bike sweat and sex."

I turned bright red, my blush practically glowing in the kitchen light. Corey, on the other hand, took it all in stride, flashing me a grin that made my heart flutter.

****

Corey grabbed me the moment we stepped into our room *and* shut the door behind us. "I like smelling your bike sweat and my cum on you pup," he admitted with a mischievous grin. "I can't help it; I guess it makes me feel like I'm marking you as mine."

I returned his eager kiss, savoring his bold honesty. But as soon as we parted, I quipped, "I think you're taking this whole 'wolf' thing maybe just a little too seriously." I chuckled, though I immediately contradicted myself by raising my arms, offering my pits to him once more, inviting him to return his muzzle to their damp, blond furriness.

He didn't hesitate to accept my invitation. "Yep, you smell like mine," he declared with a satisfied smirk before striding into the bathroom.

I started to strip down - or at least tried to. "Um, Corey? Mr. Wolf, Sir? Your latest scent marker is making my back stick to these bibs. Do you still have that tape glue remover?"

"Just get in the shower, pup," he called back. "I'll take care of you."

CHAPTER 19: CELEBRATIONS - FAMILY STYLE

Celebrations was a stately restaurant with a timeless charm, nestled on Camp Bowie Boulevard where the street was still paved with bricks. As we walked toward the entrance, Chris, clearly in love with his city, gestured toward the building and said, "This used to be the city ice house. The rails and crossbeams that moved giant blocks of ice are still intact." His pride in Fort Worth was on full display.

Corey grinned and added, "That's cool, but Dad's leaving out the best part. Celebrations serves home-cooking, farm-to-market food, family style. The side dishes are bottomless, and everyone gets their own main course. And here's the best part - you're allowed to request seconds. So, the way to play the game is, we each order something we both like, then we swap our refills. It's like a strategy game for foodies."

Ted let out a hearty laugh that could have filled the whole restaurant. "Damn Corey, it's like you're

15 again. I haven't seen you this excited about, well, *everything*, in years." He turned to me with a twinkle in his eye and added, "I think our Ollie looks good on you." Then, taking advantage of how closely I was standing next to Corey, he swept us both into one of his big fatherly bear hugs.

The food was incredible. I ordered pot roast, something that until this moment, I wasn't sure if I would ever be allowed to enjoy again. I tried to ignore the sudden unexpected pangs of homesickness it caused - a flicker of a life I'd lost. But those pangs couldn't compete with the joy of Corey giving me this amazing day. Our conversation flowed freely, as if we'd been a family all our lives. Well, I guess *they* really had been. I was just honored and grateful that they were trying their best to make sure I felt like I'd always been a part of it as well.

Right on cue, just as I finished devouring Corey's second helping of chicken-fried steak, Chris piped up with a teasing grin. "Corey, he's your puppy - you better make sure he's fed at least three times a day. It looks like he's been skipping a few meals."

I decided it was time to defend myself. "Why does everyone think I've been starving just because I was living in a car-condo?" I chuckled, making sure they knew I wasn't really offended. "I swear, I was doing fine. I was maybe eating a little too much fast food, but I wasn't wasting away."

Corey shot me a playful *I got you* look and jumped in. "And what fast-food place did you hit up most,

Ollie?" A wink sealed the setup.

I waved off his obvious ploy, genuinely confused. "Okay, I give up. Dads? What's the big deal? Why is Corey so concerned about me never having gone to Whataburger yet?"

Ted groaned dramatically, clearly taking the conversation baton. "Oh, Sport, please don't tell me you've been going to McDonald's this whole time."

"Um, no sir... mostly Wendy's?"

Ted sighed with mock exasperation. "We'll let that slide - *this time*. But only because you didn't know better." He and Corey both broke into laughter.

Chris threw me a rope and leaned in with a conspiratorial grin. "It's not really that big of a deal, Ollie. But being a regular at Whataburger? Well, it's one of the fun little ways we Texans measure just how Texan someone really is. And we're all hoping you'll want to be very Texan."

Daww. That did it. I couldn't stop the big, goofy, blushing smile that took over my face.

CHAPTER 20: REVELATIONS

Suddenly, I had an assignment again, which made me happy, but I filed it away for later. Instead, I pivoted and changed the subject. "Um, Dads, can we talk about something else Corey mentioned last night?"

Chris and Ted exchanged puzzled looks. Corey stepped in with a sheepish grin. "Okay, fine, I'll take this one. So, last night when I was helping Ollie through a bad nightmare, I called him 'my love.' I'm not taking it back, but I did say we should explain how y'all got together."

As if it were rehearsed, both dads said in unison, "You're grounded, Corey."

Completely unfazed, Corey unabashedly replied, "Dad... Ted... have I ever asked you to tell this story to anyone else before?" His tone, more serious than I'd heard it in the two short days I'd known him, seemed to catch them off guard.

Chris's expression gentled immediately as he realized his son's seriousness. "No, you haven't, Corey. I'm sorry." He turned to me, his fatherly demeanor warm and reassuring. "Ollie, this doesn't mean you have to rush into anything, and we seriously don't expect or want you to. But, here's how our story goes."

Ted began, "Chris and I had somehow never crossed paths before. And, even though DFW is a big city, the gay community here feels like a small town. So, when my friend Jeff and his husband Tom told me they wanted to introduce me to 'a big, tall Chris' at their party on Saturday, I was skeptical. I was pretty sure I'd already met all the big, tall guys in Dallas and Fort Worth."

Chris picked up the story with a warm smile. "And I was just as dubious when my friend Tom said I *had* to meet this 'muscle boy' Ted. But I trusted him enough to go. When I arrived, I was hit with a nervous energy I hadn't felt in years. And the moment Ted walked through the door, I just knew. Even though I'd never seen him before, somehow, I knew he was the one. When Tom and Jeff introduced us, all I could manage was, 'Hi, I'm Chris.'"

Ted chuckled softly, timing his words perfectly. "And I said, 'Hi, I'm Ted... and I know.'"

He sighed, giving Chris's hand a gentle squeeze, and the love between them seemed to fill the room. Even after 20 years, it was clear this story was their favorite to share, and I felt honored to witness it through their memory.

Chris continued, his voice reverent as the recollection came alive. "From that moment on, we were inseparable. We spent the whole party tucked away in a spare bedroom, just talking - pouring out our lives to each other. We followed it with a simple date, mid-week. Then, on Friday, Ted came over to meet little Corey... and, well, he basically never left. By Sunday evening, we were saying 'I love you,' and Corey was excitedly introducing Ted as his new uncle to his friends on Monday."

Ted finished his husband's thought with a knowing smile. "The point of this tale, Sport, is we've always suspected Corey had inherited another one of his father's best genes. It seems that love at first sight runs in the family. They don't do long engagements, and when they find the right person, they just... *know.*"

Chris gently took over the helm, his voice carrying the weight of a father's pride and care. "Ollie, forgive my fatherly brag, but our Corey, despite his suddenly re-invigorated teenage impulsiveness, is as solid as they come. He's steady, loyal, and prime husband material. Sure, he's dated a lot - he attracts plenty of attention - but he's never been able to settle for anything less than someone with that undeniable spark. And honestly, we've never seen him look at anyone the way he looks at you.

"So, my new son, you need to just keep taking things at your own pace. Letting yourself heal. Enjoy this new life and never feel pressured to commit to anything you're not ready for. You've been through a lot, and it's okay to let trust build slowly. But if Corey sleepily let it slip that he loves you, it's because he does. It's in his nature to be honest about his heart."

I sat there, my chest feeling impossibly full as I looked at Corey in a whole new light. My protector, my champion, my wolf. Suddenly, I saw him not just as the man who had saved me, but as the man who might be my forever.

CHAPTER 21: MOVIE NIGHT

I'm not gonna lie - Corey and I did some serious cuddling in the backseat of Chris' SUV all the way home. Let me see... I think it was several years ago - or maybe just yesterday morning, sometime around 10:00 - that I had one of my many breakdowns. That particular time, it was because I thought I had fallen for someone who couldn't possibly feel the same way about me. So, is there such a thing as mental whiplash? I happily just couldn't bring myself to worry about it at the moment.

When we got back to *my house* - lol - at 8:30, it was obvious that Corey and I had reached a whole new level of togetherness. Ted decided he needed to break our quickly strengthening spell.

"Okay, you two, I'm going to tell you an important part of the story that Corey doesn't know: you boys can't get married until you wake up together and spontaneously start singing the same song. *Your* song."

Corey looked as confused as I felt. "Dad! Uncle Ted is

confusing me."

Chris smirked. "We don't always tell you everything, my boy." I marveled at how much he sounded like Corey just then.

He continued, "But I swear, Ted and I did - we really did. All we're saying is, take your time. Listen to each other. Get in sync." He paused dramatically, and I suddenly realized he was about to pull a classic Corey move. "Also, I think we need to use the theater room. *A Quiet Place: Day One* is streaming, and I want to see it."

I swung at the softball this time. "*A Quiet Place*? Listen to each other? Corey, are our dads always so subtle?"

"Yes!" Corey high-fived me before turning to his dad with his smirk. "Dad, I get to keep him now, right?"

Ted broke in with a grin, "That's it, y'all are both on popcorn duty."

I protested, "But... We just ate. Like, a lot."

Chris rebuked with a playful twinkle in his eye, "What? You've never done dinner and a movie before? You still gotta have popcorn. And, Ollie, serious question: we absolutely trust you. Ted and I are going to have an after-dinner, pre-movie martini. Do you want anything? Corey, *you* know where the alcohol is."

It was such a casual offer, but it left me momentarily stunned. "Uh, no thanks. I'm good with popcorn and water."

Corey smiled at me, his eyes sparkling with mischief. "My boy, let's make popcorn! Dads, get your drinks ready and queue up the movie."

We made popcorn the old-fashioned way, in a covered pot with peanut oil and salt - just like my mom's father used to do with me when I was a kid. It was perfect, nostalgic, and tasted amazing, whether we were hungry or not.

The movie turned out to be surprisingly engaging. Sure, it was technically a 'horror' movie, but it became so much more. The four of us ended up snuggled into our respective mates, occasionally clutching hands during the tense moments. But what stuck with me most was how unexpectedly touching the story was. In its own way, it was a left-turn, love-at-first-sight tale at its core. The actors delivered Oscar-worthy performances, and by the end, all of us had shed a few tears.

We laughed about it afterward, teasing each other for getting emotional, but deep down, it was another shared experience that made the night unforgettable. Yet again, I found myself marveling at how impossibly incredible this day had been. I still wasn't sure it was real.

****

Corey and I made our way to our wing of the grand house, while Chris and Ted headed to theirs. The house had settled into a peaceful quiet, and it felt like the perfect ending to a perfect day. We showered together, even though cramming two big guys into a

tub-shower combo made it more awkward than grace-
ful. But the laughter and shared clumsiness made it
worth every second.

We were finally back in bed, naked and entwined,
we once again became a warm cocoon of comfort and
connection. I nuzzled into Corey's chest before teasing, "I know you were supposed to take me to a new
level again tonight, but after our epic bike adventure,
I think I'm good with just having your dick resting
between my butt cheeks again tonight. Besides, I've already got a 3:00 a.m. nightmare penciled in on our cal-
endars. You need to save your strength."

"Ollie, my boy," Corey chuckled, his voice a mix of
affection and playful mischief. "You've only gotten off
twice today. Are you sure you won't have blue balls?"

I playfully elbowed him in the stomach. "Oh, sorry!
I must've been having a bad dream."

That earned me an ambush of tickles, and it turns
out I'm outrageously ticklish. "Okay, okay, stop!" I
begged between gasps of laughter. "I'll be a good boy...
unless you're hoping for a repeat of last night's punishment."

Corey finally relented, giving me a soft kiss as he
leaned close. "Pup, you're gonna get a treat in the
morning," he murmured, his voice low and promis-
ing. "Well, at least once you're awake enough to know
it's me and remember you're safe."

As I nestled deeper into Corey's embrace, hovering
on the edge of sleep, a strange and unsettling thought

pierced through my contentment. "Corey, my inner monologue just went rogue and took a really dark turn. What if... what if I wake up in the morning back in my Bronco in a Walmart parking lot? Like all of this was just a dream that I don't get to keep?"

Corey didn't miss a beat. His arms tightened protectively around me as he whispered, "Okay, first of all, no more *Twilight Zone* for you, young man. And second, if that ever happened, I'd spend the rest of my life searching for you in every Walmart parking lot in Texas. I'll never let you go, Ollie. I promise. Goodnight, my pup."

I felt the soft press of his lips against my temple, a kiss that anchored me, as I drifted into the most peaceful, blissful sleep I'd ever known.

CHAPTER 22: BREAKFAST IN BED

After my second wonderful night in Corey's arms, I woke up at, well, oh my lurd, sometime in the morning?! It didn't look like the sun was completely up yet, but still, I'm counting this as sleeping through the whole night. Yes! I could really get used to this "no nightmares" thing.

Corey's arms tightened around me as he realized I was awake. "Hey! We made it, pup. I didn't have to dodge any punches or elbows." I could feel his smile pressed against the back of my neck, warm and reassuring. "Ollie, I wouldn't get too used to it yet. I doubt your nightmares have given up so easily, but I'll definitely take a peaceful night wrapped around you as a win. Congratulations."

As I was reveling in our surprise accomplishment, I suddenly remembered last night's conversation with the dads. "Corey, wait! This is important. Start singing whatever song is on your mind in... 3... 2... 1..."

Without missing a beat, Corey broke into: "Do-di Do-do Do-di Do-do. Pum pa pum! Pum pa deed-a-le dum!"

"Corey Allan Rainer!" Making up for skipping last night's dream battle, I twisted in his arms and gave his shoulder a light punch. "The *Twilight Zone* theme song is *not* going to be our song! Huge fail!"

We both burst into laughter, and Corey pulled me closer. "I'll admit, I was trying to play it safe," he teased, smirking.

I couldn't hold back a smile. "Dang, I feel great. I think your arms are officially the perfect therapy for me." I could barely contain my emotions; joy radiated from my face as I gazed into his sky-blue eyes. I leaned in, giving him his second morning-breath kiss of the weekend.

"Um, Ollie, I think I have a promise to keep to you this morning. Are you awake enough to accept it?" Corey's tone was soft, but there was an unmistakable glimmer of excitement behind it.

"Corey," I began, giving him my best deadpan look, "you know there's no way I have enough context to answer that, right? My handsome Mr. Cryptic." I let the moment hang before adding, "And honestly? Um, no." His face fell just a little, and I couldn't help but grin. "Well, at least not yet. Remember why we met? I gotta go try to pee. And FYI, you making my morning wood any harder isn't exactly helping. Wish me luck. What time is it, anyway? It looks really early."

"It's just before 7:00," he replied, eyes sparkling with amusement. "But I think it's going to be a cloudy day. And, pup, trust me - when you get back, you'll be very happy."

I smirked, stretching my arms lazily over my head to tease him before heading to the bathroom. Corey's wolfish chuckle followed me as I walked, proudly putting my morning *situation* on full display for my explorer, er? Maybe lover?

"Let it all out!" he called after me, his laughter warming the air between us. "Fun things await your return!"

After doing my best to empty my bladder, I happily returned to our, well, I guess we can call it our wolf den? This time, I seriously presented my pits to my alpha. "Grrr, my pup! Those are only where I'm starting." Corey dove in, sniffed, licked, and scented his beard before pulling me into a blissful morning kiss.

Locking his blue eyes with mine, his expression shifted to something very determined. "Ollie, from the moment I saw your furry taint - what, two whole days ago? - I've had one singular desire. I knew there was no way I could do it at the time, but I swear I almost begged you to let me try before I mowed your playing field." Patting the mattress, he added with a glint in his eye, "Tummy down on the bed, my Ollie. Get ready for a whole new level."

"Corey, are you really going to do what I think you said you wanted to do yesterday? Is that really a thing?"

"Trust me pup and find out." I'll never get tired of those mischievous grins.

I quickly kissed him again and rolled over with my still urgent morning wood protesting about being trapped against the mattress. I laid there with my bent elbows collapsed under my chest, slightly elevating my shoulders, waiting for what Corey was about to lead me through.

He didn't waste much time, but he did try to fake my defensive line out. He gently laid down over me and let his weight push me into the mattress. I once again felt my taint's new best friend nestle its way into its new home. Only this time, it was gently poking into my balls instead of up my crack. And he once again wrapped his arms under my chest and nuzzled his cheek next to mine. I was a bit confused but, hey, I'm totally up for a morning humping. Bed sheets are way softer than tree trunks.

After he let his weight remain on my appreciative back for only a few moments, he kissed my cheek, sighed at our impending loss of contact, and lifted his body off of mine. Wait?! I guess I'm not in for another sticky lower back...

Instead, I felt his knees settle firmly on either side of my hips, keeping me in his control as he straddled me with his hands planted beside my shoulders. A soft kiss landed at the base of my neck, and I couldn't stop the contented sigh that escaped my lips. His low growl followed in answer, sending a shiver down my spine as he began his journey south.

I was suddenly hoping, guessing, maybe even praying that I understood his intention. The first few deliberate kisses confirmed it, his lips and tongue tracing a path down each vertebra of my back. Every press of his mouth ignited a cascade of goosebumps, a ripple of sensations that left me uncontrollably quivering under his touch.

"Corey! Are you sure? Really?" My voice was shaky but full of wonder.

"Ollie pup, I absolutely am. Are you?"

I just couldn't imagine his willingness to do what I hoped he was about to do. And once again, he read my mind.

"Ollie. Don't worry, it's just skin. We showered together last night. Even so, it's the place where your scent is at its strongest. And I've already told you, there's no part of you I can resist imprinting on me. Please pup, I know you're going to love this. May I?"

I'm beginning to realize "pup" usually means *let's have fun, I got this.* It's his way of sincerely asking me to trust him. My hips involuntarily raised themselves. *Come on guys! At least try to play a little hard to get.* And his lips finally connected with the lowest part of the small of my back. I couldn't stop myself, "Corey please. Yes!" I couldn't believe that came from me.

He scooted his knees back a bit further down my thighs and he placed his hands on my butt cheeks and gently began spreading them apart, exposing my anticipating hole. "Here's our next level my boy, I know you'll like it." As he did yesterday, I felt his breath and facial hair on my cheeks and taint as a promise of where his lips were headed. But there was no further tease, just a fulfillment of that promise. I felt my man's tongue on my exposed hole and I had no choice, I had to call out, "Corey!"

"Ssshhh, pup, we may be on the far side of the house, but we still have to be a little quiet." He chuckled. "Maybe we should sleep at my house when we want to try new levels out. For right now, could you kinda snuggle your beautiful face into a pillow?" I wasn't sure how serious Corey was, but knew I didn't want him to stop. I grabbed a pillow and buried my happy face in it.

Corey lowered his whole torso down between my spread legs as his arms slid up between the mattress and my abs. His fingers found my nipples, right as his tongue started licking just above my balls then moving down my taint to rest on my quivering hole. I muffled another "Corey!" into the pillow. And he started to pleasure my hole with wide licks of his tongue. I love my dick, I've got a great one, but, damn, I'm starting to really understand just how much my ass rules my sexual world.

He never stopped bathing my hole with his tongue or kissing and licking my taint and I just kept moaning into my pillow. I have no idea how much time went by. But I still whined in protest when he pulled his arms out from under my chest and raised up from my butt. "Raise your hips, pup!" I did as Corey's elbows went over my thighs with his hands resting on my butt where they immediately started pulling my cheeks apart and his tongue got serious.

He was no longer just licking my hole; he was trying to force his tongue in to my body. I raised up higher doing my best to help him out. "Just relax your hole Ollie boy, let me in." He continued his efforts and I continued to bask in waves of unbelievable pleasure emanating from my hole. When I finally felt his tongue breach my sphincter, I was grateful that I had my pillow to muffle my moans.

Corey momentarily relented and I managed to breathe out a "Corey! That's the most amazing thing I've ever felt!" He raised up from his meal and then slowly moved his body back up mine. I turned my head out from my pillow to meet his handsome face in a kiss. I'm not going to lie, his beard and moustache smelled so much like me, I blushed.

He noticed my reaction and assured me, "Don't worry, pup. You taste delicious. Exactly like I knew you would. It's going to be so fun watching your natural furriness return to my favorite place. I'm pretty sure I'll have to check your progress several times a week.

"Let's run this into the end zone now. Why don't you roll over and move your delicious tight end to the edge of the bed?"

I couldn't stop myself in time, "Corey, I'm a wide receiver, not a tight end." Then I realized my horrible unintentional pun and we both laughed while I blushed.

I rolled and scooted to the mattress edge as he got off the bed and kneeled on the floor and helped me raise my knees to my chest. Exposing my drenched playground to my hungry wolf. "Okay pup, don't start stroking yet, let me see how close I can get you without your help."

Far be it from me to deny my explorer his new adventure. Corey's beard and moustache returned to my hole. Only this time, his fingers joined his tongue at my entrance. And after he thoroughly spit-lubed them up and rewetted my pucker, his two index fingers started taking their turns breaching my over stimulated entry. They combined forces to perform a three-way erotic dance at the gateway to my soul. I reached above my head to retrieve my trusty pillow just in time to stifle a very sincere and loud moan.

Eventually, one of Corey's fingers took the lead and dove in to play with my prostate while his tongue alternated between circling it at my hole and licking my taint all the way up to my balls. I was quickly losing control. My body was urging me to straighten my legs out to aid with my impending orgasm. I gently laid them over Corey's shoulders and tried not to shout, "Corey, don't stop! I'm about to cum. I need to touch my dick!"

Corey gazed up over my drawn-up testicles, pulsing cock, through my blond bush, and into my wide eyes and he nodded. I moved my hand to my aching dick and got maybe 5 desperate strokes in before my whole body tensed and I shot my morning load all the way over my head. Corey kept his finger on my butt button as my subsequent spurts landed on my face and chest and tummy. I swear my vision whited out during those first shots.

He gently removed his magical finger and slowly stood up between my legs. Then he leaned over my torso and started lapping my cum up as he made his way back up my body. We finally shared my latest protein shake in our kiss. I love being under Corey's weight and hairy chest. I was maybe still a bit too under the spell of my post orgasm high, but I knew what I wanted now. Maybe even needed.

"Corey? Can we sleep at your house tonight? I think I really want you to practice on me." And I gave him my best puppy dog face.

He raised up from our embrace and much to my immediate concern, he didn't return my playful look. Instead, he had the most stern fatherly look I'd ever seen on his face, it completely outclassed his serious Nurse Corey face. I was suddenly worried.

Corey noticed my fallen smile and immediately gentled his look. "Ollie, I know you were just having fun like we always do, by mentioning 'practice,' but I think we need to be serious about this. I lost my virginity as soon as I could, at a very young age. It was fun and it was with a close class mate - *no* it wasn't in the woods." He smiled to assure me he was still my Corey. "In fact, it was awesome. But it really didn't mean anything other than two boys experimenting and having a lot of fun. The most fun possible.

"At least it was until it instantly wasn't. My friend totally freaked out over what we were doing mere seconds after he shot his load hands free while my dick was still mashing his prostate. He practically ran out of the house as soon as he got his clothes back on. I was terrified I'd hurt him. Turns out, I really just scared him. He decided that he definitely wasn't gay, but I'm pretty sure he just couldn't accept how much he liked what we did. I didn't care if he was gay or not, but he totally stopped hanging out with me and I wound up losing a good friend over being too stupidly horny.

"I need you to understand something, Ollie. Being with you this weekend has given me one of the best times of my life. And you heard what Dad and Ted said about my little L-word slip early Saturday morning. I meant it, even if it accidently slipped out in a sleepy moment. I will be so honored to be your first lover. I know how *I* feel about you. I just need to know that *you* feel - or at least are starting to feel - the same way about me. As I've said before, I don't want to lose you, my Ollic. If we take things too fast and something goes so wrong that we couldn't even be close friends anymore, I don't think I could handle it."

Dammit. I'd been hoping to make it through at least one day without crying, but Corey's speech, with his sincere face and those hopeful, earnest eyes, sent tears making their familiar trek down my cheeks again. My voice was soft but steady as I answered him.

"Corey, if you remember *way* back to one of my first, way-too-frequent teary confessions, I was the one who first used the L-word - well, at least I admitted that I'd already written it into my inner monologue about you. At the time, I felt so stupid. I didn't even know you yet, at least I didn't think I did. I just knew I was so desperate to have someone to love and to love me back. And I felt childish to think that it could be you just because you were my very kind and caring nurse.

"But these past two days have been more than I ever imagined. And no, two days isn't a long time - and changing my mind in such a short time is ridiculous too. Except that it isn't, because it's different with you. I've known Ted for months, and I trust him completely. And now Chris too. I feel so loved by them - they're letting me live with them, treating me like one of their sons. And they love you, Corey. They know you better than anyone else, and *they* believe in us.

"And by the way, I honestly think they set us up on some kind of inside-out first date Friday morning. It seems so obvious. None of it was a coincidence. But look where we are now. This weekend hasn't just been the best weekend of my life - it's the start of something I never expected to find. Corey, I can't see myself ever wanting to lose you either. Even as we continue exploring, I already know where we're heading and where we'll wind up - *together*.

"So please, keep being my champion, my protector, and lead me through my most important first time. Make love to me tonight."

Corey's gaze melted, and for a moment, I'm sure I saw his eyes glisten with unshed tears. His voice was steady but thick with emotion. "Of course I will, my brave Ollie. I promise, it will be as beautiful as you are."

We kissed, deeply and without haste, until the sticky reality of our morning adventure broke our spell. Giggling as we carefully untangled ourselves, each wince and pulled chest or tummy hair a reminder of just how close we'd become.

Hand in hand, we made our way to the shower, our laughter echoing softly in the space we now shared - not just our room, but in a life we seemed to be committed to building together.

CHAPTER 23: MORNING PLANS

Instead of our customary morning "just undies" attire, Corey suggested we don shorts and tees for a special occasion. "I say we need to treat the dads to a breakfast feast," he declared with excitement. It was just after 8:30, and they'd likely be up around 9:00. Plenty of time to get the bacon sizzling, potatoes shredded, and eggs beaten. I just had one little problem...

"Corey, I don't have any normal shorts, or even swim trunks for that matter. I'm..."

As always, Corey came to my rescue. "Don't finish that thought, Ollie," he interrupted firmly, but with understanding. "It's not your fault you were kicked out of your home before you could plan outfits for every occasion. Just throw on your workout trunks. And later, since it's a cloudy and maybe rainy day, how about we go shopping? I've got someplace special in mind. Something fun and boundary-stretching," he added with a smirk.

I laughed, and decided to simply trust him. Amazed

with his easy confidence about erasing all my concerns. My boundaries were already literally and figuratively stretched out beyond my imagination. "As long as you're by my side, I'm up for more Corey fun."

With that, we made our way to the dim, still-sleeping kitchen and started bringing it to life. The sound of bacon sizzling soon filled the air, and I got to prove to my Corey that I wasn't bluffing about my cooking skills. Breakfast had always been my favorite meal to make, and I was an artist when it came to bacon: cooking it until it was perfectly crispy, yet still with just the right amount of chewy. And as for scrambled eggs? I had mastered the art of cooking them low and slow, coaxing out their over-easy flavor with lots of little soft, tasty curds.

As I sipped my sweet coffee, juggling my tasks and sneaking cuddles with Corey as often as possible, he was busy preparing the hash browns and mixing the pancake batter. The mouthwatering smell of my frying bacon did its job, rousing the Dads from their sleep. They strolled into the kitchen, pleasantly surprised by what we'd accomplished in their perfectly appointed culinary space.

Chris was the first to speak, his voice teasing, "Y'all didn't wake up singing the same song this morning, did you?"

I couldn't hold back my laughter. "Chris, your incredibly sweet and handsome son - my most likely love," I paused just long enough to read everyone's reactions, and thankfully, they all seemed accepting, "started 'do-do-doing' the theme from *The Twilight Zone.* So, naturally, I had to three-name him and punch his shoulder."

The kitchen erupted in laughter, and Uncle Ted was the first to recover. "Corey, you're a brilliant nurse and a brilliant man period. But have you ever considered just *asking* Ollie what kind of music he likes? Son, Let's not make this any harder than it has to be."

I'm not sure I'd seen Corey blush that brightly before, but oh, it was an enlightening sight to behold. It's not that I wanted to see my man embarrassed - it's just good to know his dads can make him feel as adorably flustered as he makes me feel sometimes.

Corey, always quick on his feet, managed to brush off the rebuke with his usual charm. "Funny you should ask that, Uncle Ted. We're making the best of this rainy day with a little Dallas shopping excursion, and I was planning on asking him that very question on the way over. My pup here needs proper swimming attire and some casual shorts. I don't think he quite understood what appropriate 'Texas summer' attire was when his father rushed his packing." He gave my neck a playful squeeze and pulled me into a hug, leaving me smiling and blushing in equal measure.

Ted made an unexpected pivot in our conversation, his tone shifted, more serious than I was expecting. "Ollie, I know I'm beating a dead horse - unnecessarily - but Sport, do you have any idea just how brutal Texas summers can get? Even up here in 'North' Texas? How were you planning on sleeping in your car - with the windows up to protect you - when the overnight lows start hitting 85 degrees?"

He saw the sudden flash of shame on my face, and before I could retreat back into Corey's arms, he gently pulled me into his own. His voice becoming it's most fatherly, "It's okay, Sport. I just can't believe you didn't realize how much I cared about you, or understood that I knew you had to be struggling." His embrace tightened, "I should've stepped in sooner. I swear, pup, I'm really just mad at myself, not you."

"I'm sor -" Corey's hand on my shoulder stopped me mid-apology. His steady presence gave me the courage to answer, "I was scared, sir. I thought if I asked for help - if people found out what was really going on - I could lose my job, along with any chance of continuing on with my life. My Father isn't taking me back. I couldn't see any other way forward, so I just kept going and hoped for the best."

I glanced down into Ted's gaze and saw tears shimmering in his eyes. Wanting to reassure him, I added, "And let's face it, Dad - this is the best 'best' I could've ever imagined."

Corey let me have my moment with my new dad and stayed at the stove, vigilantly keeping watch over the hash browns and pancakes.

Chris quietly joined our hug, his arms encircling both of us. His words were simple, yet they carried the weight of everything I didn't know I needed to hear. "We love you too, pup."

****

It was finally time for breakfast! I'm not sure our spread could match the bold delight of Sam's Benedict, but everything was perfect and delicious. We all sat around the nook table, eating and laughing as we got to know each other even better. I couldn't resist asking, "So, did Corey really decide to use the oven as a kiln and try to bake clay fossils into stone?"

Chris laughed and motioned his fork at me. "Just keep doing that Ollie. Keep sharing all your ridiculous stories. You'll find your song."

As we finished up and began cleaning the table, Corey casually dropped our news. "Hey, I think Ollie should spend the night at my house tonight. I mean, it makes sense since I'm taking him to the doctor in the morning, and his office is closer to me than y'all."

Ted raised an eyebrow, his tone laced with playful skepticism. "And that's your story?"

I decided it was my turn to step in and set things straight. "No, sir. The truth is, I made a big request of Corey this morning. It took a little while, but I convinced him I really meant it." Corey glanced at me, his expression filled with pride and respect, and I felt my heart swell in response, knowing I'd made the right move.

Our dads looked at us with a mixture of concern, curiosity, and - was that a look of pride? Chris broke the silence, his voice stern but full of parental care, "Are you absolutely sure? Both of you?"

This time, Corey and I got to answer in unison, our resolve clear: "Yes, we are."

I took a deep breath and continued, "Chris, Ted, I know I'm a bit... well, touch-starved. And I know I'm still going to have plenty of nightmares on my journey, but I also know I'm really falling in love with Corey - and with you two, too. I want this. I think I even need it right now. I mean, I'm 19, and I'm pretty sure that makes me the world's oldest gay virgin." I paused, hoping to earn a laugh, and I wasn't disappointed. Their chuckles eased the knot in my chest.

"But seriously, I understand a weekend is a ridiculously short time, but you've all made me feel like I belong. And I trust Corey. Even if things don't work out - and honestly, I don't think there's any way that could happen - I know he'll still be the best first I could ever ask for. Please... do we have your blessing?"

Their answer didn't come in words but in action: another Family Hug of Acceptance, warm and all-encompassing. Depending on how you looked at it, it was either the most inappropriate moment for one - or the most perfect moment imaginable.

CHAPTER 24: DALLAS ATTITUDE

First off, have I mentioned how much I love riding in Corey's Mach E? The instant acceleration feels like a perfect metaphor for our relationship - fast, electric, and full of momentum. Even the bumps in the road seem smoother, easier to endure with him at the wheel. We headed east to Dallas under cloudy skies that threatened rain but never quite followed through. With Corey driving and me finally stress-free, it was like seeing this world for the first time, even though I'd driven this same road just two days ago.

Arlington came into view like an exploded Disneyland for sports and thrills. Jerry's World - home of the Cowboys - loomed like a monument to NFL excess. Not to be outdone, The Ranger's home, Globe Life Field, had its insanely over-engineered movable roof. Finally, Hurricane Harbor and the world's original Six Flags gave thrill-goers the opportunity to choose their favorite coaster: Wet or dry.

The overwhelming sight made me give an astonished grin, "Unless you want to, I promise not to make you set through a football game - like we could even get tickets - but we absolutely have to ride those coasters!" Corey's enthusiastic nod told me he was already on board.

A few minutes later as we crested the final rise before entering Dallas on I-30, I realized the freeway gave the Big D skyline a "hero's shot" the same, yet completely different from, the one it gives Fort Worth. It was grand, sprawling, and unapologetically *big*. Everything about it seemed designed to assert itself as bigger, brighter, and bolder than its western neighbor. If Fort Worth felt like a warm handshake, Dallas was an entrance fanfare.

Watching Corey navigate the downtown Dallas labyrinth of freeways, I was grateful he was behind the wheel. The maze of ramps, fly-overs, merges and exits felt like a challenge for only the brave or the local. Eventually, we made our way up Central Expressway to NorthPark Center, where I quickly learned that Dallasites carry an attitude to match their skyline - bold, confident, and just a bit overwhelming. But with Corey by my side, I couldn't help but embrace it all.

As we entered a high-end department store, I hesitated, suddenly nervous about spending any money. "Um, Corey, everything here is really going to cut into my back-to-school budget. Maybe we should go exploring at the nearest Target or Walmart? I know where the best ones are."

"Ollie, I swear I'm not buying *your* love." He gave me a knowing smile. "But I'm definitely buying anything *my* love wants. Is that okay?"

I couldn't help but blush - and grin. I'm so falling in love with him and his cheesy lines. He tilted my chin up and kissed me softly.

I glanced around, suddenly aware of the people shopping around us. "Um, is this okay? I mean, this mall is pretty crowded, and it seems a bit... family-oriented."

"Believe me, it's NorthPark. Just don't let me catch you cruising the main floor men's room off the east main entrance." His smirk was impossible to figure out if he was being serious, and honestly, I didn't care - I *have* my man.

By the end of our spree, I had four pairs of shorts, five new short-sleeved shirts, and my first-ever stash of nine pairs of tighty-whities for coffee and breakfast with the family. I couldn't thank Corey enough, and I wasn't sure how to even begin to try.

As we browsed through another store, I remembered the conversation we were supposed to have. "So, Corey... what kind of music do you like?"

Corey looked at me, also remembering our assignment. "I'm a product of being super close with my dad - I honestly love 80s and 90s alternative. How about you?"

I absolutely beamed. "Same! Does this mean we're getting close?"

"Well, pup, it means we're playing on the same field." He shot me a playful grin. "Now let's go complete your summer wardrobe. I've got a fun store in Oak Lawn in mind."

"What's Oak Lawn?"

He gave me an evil smirk that sent a thrill through me. "It's Dallas' incarnation of 'Boys' Town.' It's their gayborhood. You ready?"

I had no idea what was waiting for me, but I knew one thing for sure - Corey was about to stretch my boundaries again. And I hoped I was ready for it.

CHAPTER 25: THE PROMISED LAND

Instead of freeways, Corey took the scenic route from NorthPark to the fabled "promised land" of Oak Lawn - offering me a glimpse of Dallas at its most opulent along the way. He warned me not to get overwhelmed by what I was about to see. And damn - if I thought my new neighborhood was beautiful, Highland Park was straight out of a dream. It didn't even seem real, and Corey, with a chuckle and eye-roll, he assured me it wasn't.

"This is the Beverly Hills of Dallas," he explained, as we passed endless manicured lawns of sprawling estates. "In fact, I should've taken you down Beverley Drive, where the poor houses start at twenty million. Oh, and fun fact - we just passed Jerry Jones' mansion, right back there when we crossed Armstrong. Don't give it too much credence, though. Now that I have you, real Dallas, real Fort Worth, the whole Metroplex, means way more to me than all of this pretense."

"Dang, my man, you and your beautiful, cheesy lines," I said, beaming. "Do you use them on all your dates?"

Corey shoved my shoulder, grinning. "Nope. Just on the boy I love." Before I could melt, he changed the subject. "Hey, I know we had a big breakfast, but before you model sexy speedos for the world, how about a little lunch?"

I gave him a soft shove back - I mean, he was driving after all. "Okay, I have absolutely no idea what I should be expecting, *or dreading.* But if I'm going to be the least bit naked in front of anyone, let's just rip the speedo-modeling Band-Aid off *before* we eat again. Deal?"

Corey chuckled. "'As you wish.'" He glanced at me with a loving wink. "By the way, have you ever watched *The Princess Bride*?"

"Duh. I do - or did - have a really wonderful grandfather, so yeah, I've seen it. And I appreciate the thought."

I couldn't help but give my Corey another hero worshiping gaze.

****

We turned right onto a new street, and my sense of direction - already questionable - was now completely lost. The closer we got to downtown Dallas, the more the streets seemed to change names and directions like they had something to hide. But then, I saw them: rainbow stripes painted across every crosswalk. The first street sign I finally paid attention to, read "Cedar Springs," and I noticed Gay Pride flags fluttering proudly from the buildings lining the street. It finally hit me - this was as sacred ground to us LGBTQIA+ folks as TCU stadium was to my football soul.

Corey noticed my wide-eyed wonder. "Yes, my baby gay," he said, voice dripping with warm humor, "there are a lot of us gay Texans here in the Metroplex. Even more if we ever explore Houston. Welcome to your homeland, my son." He barely got the last part out - sorry - with a straight face.

While we were laughing at Corey's hokey travelogue, we made a quick left at a light before immediately pulling into a parking space right in front of a store called *Skivvies*.

After letting my initial impression of the place soak in, I nervously uttered, "Uh, Corey? You already bought me plenty of new underwear. I'm good. Really." Unsure if I actually wanted to get out of the car.

Corey squeezed my knee, once again, reassuring me. "Ollie, my sweet, clueless pup," his adorable smirk and wink told me he wasn't too serious about that slight. "This isn't about more tighty-whities. We're here to get you some appropriate pool side swimwear. Believe me, *Skivvies* is the place for gay pups like you to go. I swear, thirty years from now, you'll be telling this story to all of our baby gay friends. Just trust me, okay? The people here are wonderful - friendly, helpful, and *fun*."

I still hesitated but let him coax me out of the car and up to the storefront. It was as overwhelmingly strange as the urology clinic's "chamber of horrors" was on Friday morning, but I had to admit, in a completely different and intriguing way. The mannequins in the window were dressed - or, more accurately, *undressed* - in leather straps, tiny leather shorts or jocks, and all kinds of other accessories I'd only seen in gay porn fantasies. I shamelessly grabbed Corey's arm and held on like my life depended on it.

He smiled over at me, his voice sincere and steady. "I got you, my pup. I swear, everything's alright."

As soon as we opened the door and stepped inside, two very attractive guys behind the sales counter turned to watch us enter. One looked about Chris and Ted's age, while the other seemed closer to Corey's. The older one greeted us with a warm, knowing smile.

"Corey! Great to see you! How are your dads? Are you here to pick up a new suit for pool season?" Then his eyes landed on me, still holding Corey's arm. His eyebrows arched just enough to make me feel like I was being assessed. "Or... maybe something else?"

Corey replied with a hearty laugh. "Justin! I was hoping you'd be working today. It's great to see you again. The dads are doing great and I'm all set for swimwear, but my man Ollie here..." he squeezed my shoulders with pride, "...just realized he'd packed for his long visit without bringing anything appropriate to wear to the pool. He's living with my dads for the summer and, well, had no idea what the dress code was."

Justin gave me a once-over that felt just a little too familiar, his tone light but slightly teasing. "Lucky pup."

I decided I wasn't just going to stand there blushing. I stepped forward and extended my hand. "Nice to meet you, Justin." I shook his hand firmly, catching his mildly stunned expression. "Ted is my amazing mentor at work, and Chris is one of the kindest people I've ever met. They've been incredible to me - like fathers. I'd really like something appropriate for their pool this summer."

Justin's demeanor shifted immediately, his smile turning more genuine as he reassessed me. "Alright, Ollie, let's make sure you look amazing and make Fort Worth proud. Killer trunks, coming right up."

Before I could even take in the full glory of the wall of provocative swim trunks ahead of us, he'd already rattled off my correct waist size and handed Corey at least six pairs of trunks. Meanwhile, I just stood there in awe, feeling like I'd entered some alternate universe where speedo-cuts were the ultimate formal wear.

Justin guided us toward the most unapologetically exposed changing rooms I'd ever seen. They opened directly into the store's main shopping floor - and front door - with a swinging saloon-style door offering a precarious semblance of privacy - emphasis on "semblance." Maybe - just barely - say between 2:30 and 4:00 on a clock face, the stalls gave some modesty, but they absolutely provided a stage for any shoppers with a desire to strut their stuff.

Corey leaned over and murmured into the curls covering my ear, "It's all just for fun, I promise." At least he didn't repeat Friday's sound bite, *Turn around and be proud.* That's something, I guess. With a deep breath, I ducked into the stall, peeled off my jeans and dropped my undies, then slid the first pair of trunks up my furry, beefy thighs. The fabric clung tightly, showcasing a bit more than I'd bargained for. After a quick adjustment to ensure I was tucked and decent - or as decent as these trunks would allow - I called over the stall door, "Corey, what do you think?"

Before Corey could reply, Justin chimed in, "Oh no, no, no, Ollie! You can't tell anything while standing in there with your shirt on. Take it off and come out here. Trust me, once you're out here in the open, then we'll know if the trunks work."

I hesitated, glancing at Corey, who promptly chuckled and covered his face with one hand in his familiar gesture of not-so-sincere shame, while the other hand gave me an exaggerated thumbs-up. I glared at him through the door. *He's enjoying this way too much.* I resolved to punch him later - *twice.* Still, I felt his unspoken encouragement and figured, hey, it's going to be a fun story for our grandkids. Gathering my nerve, I pulled my shirt off, swallowed my doubts, and stepped out.

The second I emerged, every guy in the store stopped what they were doing and started applauding. My face instantly burned hotter than the Texas sun. And Corey? My man was grinning like he'd just won the lottery - until his expression shifted. He wasn't laughing. He wasn't smirking. His jaw had gone slack, and his wide eyes reflected something raw and honest.

My Norse God was stunned by me? That realization hit harder than any spontaneous applause from friendly strangers. Elation carried me across the floor to the full-length mirror *conveniently located...* in the middle of the room. Because, of course, that's exactly where it had to be.

I repeated the same routine with three more pairs of trunks, stepping out to another round of applause each time. Justin and Corey had a good-natured debate over which two trunks I should get. Naturally, the debate ended with Corey's trademark smirk and Justin's appraising grin as they regarded my still mostly naked form and concluded, "Why not all four?" After all, the Texas summer is long, hot, and filled with pools waiting to be graced by my presence - or so they claimed.

We said our goodbyes with warm hugs - I mean, come on, after baring pretty much everything to Justin and a room full of strangers, a hug felt practically formal. Corey ushered me out the door with his usual confident charm, and as we walked to the car he furrowed his brow and asked, "Okay, Ollie, what sounds better right now? A great burger or some fantastic fried chicken?"

I laughed at his seriousness over such a decision, but I didn't hesitate. "Burger, please!" We quickly stowed my latest purchases in the frunk of his Mach-

E, and then wandered down the rainbow-clad sidewalk. We passed bars and clubs that I'd have to wait a couple of years to step into legally, but I didn't feel like I was missing out. By the time we reached the burger joint and sat down for my first great gay Texan meal, I realized I'd just had one of the most unforgettable days of my life with my super hero and co-explorer by my side.

CHAPTER 26: THUNDERSTORMS AND PIZZA

We definitely didn't drive back to Fort Worth in silent reverie. I was totally stoked about the day and made sure Corey knew it. "I can't believe I just modeled speedos in front of a whole store full of gay guys. I mean… they were gay, right?"

Corey chuckled sweetly; his voice full of amused affection. "Yes, my pup, they were all *probably* gay."

He let me babble on for the entire drive back, listening patiently as I processed every moment of our adventure. As we descended into Fort Worth, its familiar skyline came into view, and I decided to share something deeper. "Corey, this view of Fort Worth was my first real assurance that I'd somehow be okay. I mean, if a city could have this amazing, welcoming shot, how could I not be?" My voice wavered a little, and I swallowed down the emotion rising in my throat.

Corey glanced over at me with a soft expression. "I love seeing my city through your eyes, Ollie. You make everything feel shiny and special. Don't ever lose that, pup. It's a gift."

We reached Corey's cottage just as the heavens decided to finally open up. I'd experienced a few Texas thunderstorms at night, alone in my Bronco, and learned that they weren't kidding around. But now, standing inside Corey's perfectly comforting home, the storm felt different. It wasn't something to fear - it was cozy, almost romantic, setting the stage for what came next.

"Ollie," Corey started, his tone light, "I know you haven't seen much of my house yet - and hey, *Ted* knows that too - but believe me, it's all recently remodeled. My, er, *our*?" His hopeful gaze met mine, and I immediately nodded. "*Our* kitchen is more than a match for Dad and Ted's. I know we could cook something amazing, but..." He let out a small laugh, "it's been another long day in an extremely long and wonderful weekend. How about we just Netflix and chill... and order pizza?"

I happily agreed, and Corey gave me my first real tour of his sweet home. It was completely different from Chris and Ted's expansive house. Corey's place couldn't have been more than 2,500 square feet, with three cozy bedrooms and two perfectly updated bathrooms. No wonder he took me to a '50s-style diner for our first meal - this was the perfect mid-century home, beautifully modernized for a 2020's lifestyle.

The tour only got better when Corey led me out to the covered patio overlooking the backyard. There wasn't a dramatic cliff face for privacy, but it didn't need one. Corey's retreat felt just as secluded; with the most elegantly styled pool I'd ever seen. Chris and Ted's pool was big, bold, and unmistakably Texan. Corey's was smaller, serene, and absolutely fit the house perfectly. And I loved it.

All I could manage to say was, "No wonder Ted knew I hadn't seen your pool. Corey, this is amazing - even in the storm."

We returned to the living room, and despite the temptation, somehow managed to keep our clothes on until the pizza arrived, though they definitely ended up a bit disheveled. The delivery driver got an extra-big tip for braving the rain.

I never knew I was a fan of thin crust pizza until Corey handed me a slice of what he'd ordered. It was perfect, just like everything else about the whole day. After we finished eating, we curled up on the couch together, the sound of the storm wrapping around us. I melted into his arms, feeling completely safe, utterly content, and maybe just a little nervous as I thought about what I'd asked him to do tonight.

Corey seemed to once again sense my thoughts. He gently tilted my chin up to meet his gaze, his voice tender. "My Ollie, are you still sure about what you asked this morning?"

I started shivering, the anticipation and emotion washing over me. But I found my voice, steady enough to whisper, "Yes, sir."

CHAPTER 27: THE FIRST VERSE OF US

"Um, Corey? I've been worried about something. You, well, you know that thing you did to me before you had to shave my crack? Do we need to do that again? I want my first time to be awesome, not embarrassing."

"Ollie, you're young, and, well, very regular. If you feel comfortable right now, then there's a 99% chance that everything is absolutely fine. I only did that because of the risk of infection from the shaving. For what we're about to do? Don't worry. Plus, I think we're comfortable enough to stop and regroup after any unexpected 'fabulous surprises.'" I loved his corny grins.

"Cool, but I really kinda liked you inserting that nozzle while holding me upright in your arms." I'm not sure my attempt at pillow talk landed as well as I had hoped.

Corey covered for me, "Oh my Ollie! We can definitely do that position again except with *my* nozzle being inserted into your butt." He stood up from our couch snuggling and offered me his hand. I took it and allowed him to lead me to his, maybe one day *our,* bedroom. I hate to say it, but once again, it's *Go Time.*

We stepped into his warmly lit alpha wolf den, and I swear it felt like the room itself was welcoming me, whispering promises of safety and belonging. I loved my bedroom at Chris and Ted's house, but here, in Corey's home, I could hear something deeper - a call to stay, to make this my forever. We stood in the room's soft glow, our eyes locking, and I saw nothing but love and hope reflected in his. I willed him to see the same in mine - love, longing, and the trust I'd finally found in him.

Leaning into each other, our lips met in a kiss that was soft yet deliberate. This wasn't the desperate frenzy of unbridled passion, not yet. Corey was guiding us, keeping the flames low, letting them build slowly. This was our moment to savor. This was our time to remember forever.

As our kisses deepened, our hands began to explore. We started undressing each other with the careful reverence of two people unwrapping a gift. Corey, ever confident and composed, had already perfected the art of unbuckling my belt in one swift motion. I wasn't quite as practiced, but my eagerness more than made up for it. My pants hit the floor first, but his joined mine just moments later, as if we were in perfect synchronization. We stepped free of the fabric pooling at our feet and fell back into each other's arms, our embrace tighter now, our hearts beating in unison. Once more, our cocks were battling for dominance against our lower abdomens. I didn't care about the outcome; I knew we'd both be victorious in the end.

Corey's now-familiar move had my shirt slipping over my head in one fluid motion, and I knew what was coming next. His face dipped toward my pits, and I wasn't disappointed. Damn, I'm grateful guys get to grow beards. He allowed me to return the favor but before I could simply scent my beard in his, he gently lifted my arm again, raising his own in turn. For a moment, we stood there, leaning into each other, exploring in perfect reciprocity. It was primal, intimate - an unspoken offering of our truest, rawest selves. *This is me. Is that okay?* The answer was in every breath we took: *Yes. And this is me.* In that exchange, we weren't just two people anymore; we were one.

Fully nude and finally back into our embrace, Corey knew that I was still depending on him to stay in the lead, and he didn't fumble. He broke our kiss long enough to efficiently strip his bed down to the pillows and sheet. Then just like on Friday, he picked me up into his arms with his bigger body, and gently lowered me onto his bed. I scooted over to lay in the middle. Corey jumped on board, crawled above me and straddled my crotch.

With a loving, yet slightly wolfish smirk, he took my hands in his and gently forced my arms above my head, his favorite position to have me in. I helped him by moving them together over my head. He appreciated my offer and only used one hand to keep them both there. His free hand immediately made it down to my throat as he feverishly kissed my mouth and then alternated between licking either pit. Only to return again to my mouth to deliver his scented beard.

"Ollie, I. Love. You. You don't have to say it back - I just need you to know it. I've known about you longer than you've known about me, and every moment since has led me here to you. Remember that trust thing? I need you to trust me now. You're so beautiful and special, and I'm probably going to start stumbling over my words because of how deeply I feel for you and need what we're about to do. But I swear, I'll always be listening. You'll always be in control. If I sense even a flicker of fear or hesitation, I'll stop immediately. I promise. Okay?"

I already knew that implicitly, but damn. It was a beautiful confession. I was already uncontrollably shivering again. I was prepared for his next request. "Ollie, rollover pup, face down, ass up." I chuckled at his reference to the first time he jokingly gave me that instruction. This time, I understood how *not* demeaning and completely serious his request was.

I excitedly rolled over under him and was quickly rewarded by the feeling of his very hard cock once again sliding into my crack. But that wasn't the game this time. Unlike this morning, he immediately slid his hips down my legs as his hands and face dove into my crack like he was a man, wait, *wolf*, possessed. I've only ever been rimmed twice and while the first time was an incredible introductory course, this was a master class.

Even better, this time I didn't have to mute my audio commentary. "Corey! Fuck! I mean, fuck! Damn, Corey! Fuck, yes. Corey, please. Fuck!" Lurd... I chuckled in the realization that my unpracticed baby gay "sex talk" was probably way better off left muted. From that outburst on, I tried to limit myself to making the sexiest moans and growls I could muster. Hey, I was a work in progress.

Corey didn't seem to mind my incoherent babble and eagerly continued his ministrations. And once more, his fingers joined the fray and I was enjoying the experience of being slowly opened up. I loved every stretch! Once more, I realized my butt definitely ruled my world.

Corey sobered up for just a few moments and asked a question I wasn't prepared for. "Ollie, I'm a pretty big guy, I have, well, *toys*... I could use them to open you up a little bit at a time. It'll definitely make our final goal easier. Would you like me to get them? I'm sure it'll be damn fun for both of us."

It was my turn to be animalistic, "Corey! Do not leave my ass right now. We're going to have an absolute blast playing with your toys - *later*. I know I probably don't understand exactly what I'm getting into, but right now, my Norse God, I don't want anything inside my hole unless it's a part of your body. Well, and lube... Lots of lube would probably be great." I suddenly understood that for me and Corey, laughter has got to be a big part of our love making.

We both chuckled like high school boys, but Corey took the opportunity to turn it in to a fun new mini level. "Deal, but we're gonna make lube prep just as fun as toy prep." He put two pillows under my hips and said, "Stay! Good pup! Stay!" As if I had any desire to move. He reached over into his nightstand and retrieved a nearly full bottle of lube. Ha! I liked that it was nearly full. Now all I needed to do was figure out how long ago he bought it.

"Here we go pup." And I felt my favorite fingers push my cheeks apart again and instead of spit, I felt the viscous and cool lube drizzle down over my hole. It kept slowly dripping and driving me wild until those favorite fingers switched roles and started showing the lube the way into my inner sanctum. Once more, my body reacted on my behalf and my hips shot up. I heard an almost mandatory, "There's my good pup. He knows what he wants and how to get it."

One finger became two and more lube joined the party. My hole was having its own little quivering meltdown, and after a third finger entered me and found my prostate, I suddenly stopped quivering and nearly screamed, "Fuck! Yes! Please Corey! Fuck me!" Oops, my bad, I was eminently grateful for Corey's wisdom of taking this to his house.

Corey chuckled sinisterly, "Calm down pup, that's exactly what I'm about to do, but I'm happy you told me just how ready you are. As much as I want to mount you just like this, as animalistic as possible; I love you pup, and I want this to feel good for you every step of the way. I don't want your inner monologue to have to write, 'The sudden pain was beyond belief but then slowly, it turned into pleasure.' Not for my pup, *my love*. I need you to roll over. Exactly where you are, with your hips on the pillows."

I most ungracefully wormed over in place and realized how sweaty we both were already. It only added to the perfect atmosphere. My sexually aromatic pits danced with Corey's. There was no battle for dominance, we both knew which dancer was leading and which one was following. The choreography was simply moving us to our shared desire.

He raised my knees over his shoulders and placed his ever-alert cock head right at my willing entrance. He applied just enough pressure to make sure it wouldn't stray from its target and then gave all his attention to me. "Ollie, we don't have to finish this way, but it's how we need to get started. I want to see your face and be able to react to every emotion I see you expressing. Are you okay my beautiful boy?"

Damn, I didn't think I could beam any brighter. I simply said, "Yes my wolf, I need you in me."

This time it was Corey's turn, "Pup, we really need to work on your sex talk." Damn it's amazing to feel so comfortable to be able to laugh with your lover even when it's just seconds before the single most intimate moment of your life. And Corey commandingly, but gently, thrust his hips forward and things got serious.

"Ollie, for once in my life, I absolutely wish I had a standard sized cock. But I don't. Neither of us do. But I've got you. Just keep looking at me. Tell me everything you feel, verbally or just with your face. I need you to be absolutely here with me for these first few moments. You can start writing your glorious inner monologue after we're coupled and I start fucking you into a blissful stupor.

"Remember when I had to ask you that stupid question on our first morning? 'Do you have any questions?'. Well, this command is just as dumb. Just relax your hole, and try to push out a bit. Here we go pup." His very serious face didn't really convey the humor of his statement but I tried my best to comply with his request.

I felt a sudden, um, "pop?" I don't know why I felt it that way, but it was like a hollow feeling. Like a part of me that I'd never known was missing, was suddenly fitting into a blank space in my puzzle that it always should have been in. And I was shocked to my core. It wasn't really painful; it was more like a feeling of fulness that I instantly feared would drown me forever in its exquisiteness. I gave the most honest gasp of my life.

As usual, Corey read my mind. "That's it Ollie; I got you in so many new ways right now. You can't run away, just relax and let me have what you're willing to give. Just keep relaxing." He didn't attempt to push in any further, happy with his current 3-inch beach head. He gazed into my wide eyes and kissed me deeply once again. Not aggressively, we weren't ready for that, just passionately with yet another promise of more to come.

As we continued our kiss, I just barely noticed, in an almost subconscious way that his amazing cock had slowly kept making its way into my deepest being. By the time he released me from his spell, several minutes had gone by and he gleefully declared, "You've taken all of me my pup, my pubes are warming your testicles. Are you okay?"

"Corey, fuck, I've never felt this way in my life. You can't ask a dog to describe a rainbow. My brain is exploding with colors I've never seen before. But, Damn! I do know you are deep!"

Corey gently started slowly sawing his cock in and out just a few times. It felt amazing, *mostly*. But every time he bottomed out, I have to admit it didn't feel great. Corey immediately read my face.

"It's okay, I'm a big boy, remember? At least I was able to get all of me inside you while I got to watch your beautiful face. I'm afraid it'll take a lot more *practice*," - my poor unknowing cousin - "before I get to breed you while looking into your eyes. Practice that I can't wait to implement a strict regime for as soon as possible. But for tonight, I'm going to slowly, *very* slowly, pull out then I want you to roll over again. I'm going to mount you from behind. All you need to do is flex those incredible glutes of yours to keep me from going too deep while still allowing me to lose myself in the field I was born to play in."

Corey paused, "Ollie, I just have one more very serious question left. You understand that dad and Ted know exactly what we're doing tonight. Don't think for a moment that they'd let it happen if they didn't expect me to be a gentleman. So, when the time comes, do you want me to pull out? Or do you want me to get you pregnant with our puppies? I don't think I'll be able to ask again once we start, please let me know now."

I kept trying to blind my lover with my smile. "Corey, for two days now, having your puppies is all I've thought about. You've been so tender and metered leading me through our explorations and I absolutely needed that. But my man, I'm ready to be all yours." I rolled over once more, thrilled to give every aspect of my virginity to him. "Corey, it's my turn for a cheesy line: Breed me and make me yours."

As I was rolling over, the storm raging outside decided to join our passion with gusto. Pounding rain with intense lightning and thunder assaulted the house. I suddenly remembered my father's fear of turbulent weather, but his fear isn't mine. He left me stranded and without guidance, to be adrift in a world I wasn't prepared for. Yet I still managed to persevere every storm alone. Until my Norse God, um, God of Thunder, found me.

I surrendered to my latest epiphany; Corey and his dads were all I needed. And I mind-bogglingly craved Corey to completely make me his more than ever before. I howled every bit as sincerely as he did on our little manhole cover mountain top, as he re-entered me and started his rut. I was at an unimagined new level. One I fear very few lovers get to experience.

Like our tree-time yesterday, he hooked his arm under my pit and his hand moved to my neck. I absolutely loved the primitiveness of it and instinctively tilted my head to meet his hungry kiss. His heavy and hard cock was rapidly moving in and out of my over stimulated hole and every time it mashed past my prostate, I moved a rung higher to my climax. My hips eagerly rose up to meet his thrusts. He had taught me well over our short weekend together. Every thrust was ecstasy. I had no idea my body could feel so much pleasure.

As the lightning and thunder intensified, Corey's motions started to lose their commanding cadence. His thrusts became more ragged and shallow as he started trying to stay as deep in me as possible. I knew that meant he was getting close. His hand tightened around my chest and throat and our kiss was again lost as our temples pressed into each other so hard it was as if we were trying to become one.

My climax was only ahead of his by a few intense moments, I shuttered and delivered my load onto Corey's sheets and I let an incredulous "fuck" slip from my lips. I pressed my hips up into his body, relaxed my glutes to let him go as deep as he needed. I swear I felt his cock grow even larger as he delivered his seed deep into my soul. I could feel his warmness spread throughout my body. I was happier than I'd ever been in my newly amazing life.

I was bathed in Corey's sweat as it dripped down and mixed with my own. While we were panting and basking in our post orgasmic coupling, he sweetly but unnecessarily asked, "Ollie, I have no words to describe what just happened, and, um, that was the most intense experience I've ever had. But, well, do we need to take care of you now?"

It was my turn to let him feel my chuckle through my chest. "Corey, my love, just stay inside me as long as you can. I never want to feel empty and alone again. And, well, the sheets under my very satisfied dick are the only thing you need to worry about tonight... because I ain't sleeping in the wet spot." And we burst into another fit of no longer embarrassing giggles.

CHAPTER 28: OLLIE'S HEART

Lying here gazing at the ceiling of Corey's bedroom, listening to the calming rhythm of the storm outside, I felt more at peace than I ever thought possible. I finally knew why my cousin liked "practicing" so much. And knowing that I currently had millions of little Coreys swimming inside me, gave me the most unexpected warm and loved feeling. It didn't hurt that my man had his big arm draped across my chest, his beard nuzzled between my neck and shoulder, and his furry quad laid over my upper thighs, just touching the bottom of my ball sac. As if he were keeping his mate still to make sure our mating would be successful.

He began nibbling at my ear, his voice soft and full of emotion. "I love you, Ollie. You're mine forever, and I'm yours for as long as you'll have me."

I happily said it again, "I love you too Corey." Then, with a playful glint in my eye, I added, "If that's what sex is always going to be like, I'm not sure forever is gonna be long enough." I hugged his shoulder in tighter to mine and continued. "By the way, I'm absolutely loving exploring our bedroom at Chris and Ted's. Lurd, 9-year-old Corey between his two hot dads is my favorite picture. If we'd have grown up together, I'm pretty sure I would have gotten you to practice with me by age 15."

Corey snorted; his smirk again full of mischief. "Ollie, you were 6 when I was 15, and I was 24 by the time you were, let's just not go there."

I rolled my eyes, laughing softly. "You know that's not even what I mean, right?"

Corey booped my nose, his playful grin softening into something tender. "I just wish I could see your baby and grade school pics. I'm sure I would've instantly fallen in love with my little pup back then too."

A pang hit me as I replied, "I'm sure my dad has probably thrown them all out or burned them by now. I still don't understand why me being gay made him hate me so much. I mean, I still try my best to love him."

Corey's expression shifted, his forehead gently pressing to mine. He looked at me with something close to awe, mixed with frustration. "Ollie, maybe he doesn't hate you. Maybe he hates himself. Maybe there's something inside him that's broken, something he can't fix or face. But I've gotta say, that man pisses me the fuck off. If I ever meet him, he'll be the one on the floor with a bloody nose."

I couldn't help but grin. "Grrr! My wolf protector."

Corey chuckled at my growl, but his voice softened,

brushing against something deeper. "Always, pup."

I felt the smile on my face grow, my nose lightly bumping his. "You know, in a really bass-ackwards way..."

"Bass-ackwards?" Corey interrupted, his brow raised, the tiniest smirk tugging at the corner of his lips.

"Hey, I still don't like cussing, well, I make exceptions when your cock is in my colon."

"I wasn't that deep, boy; I went easy on you. We still have so many more levels and fun positions to explore."

"Um, I think I'll be the judge of how deep you were, and I'm pretty sure I have a few of your swimmers currently planning an expedition to my esophagus to prove it," I teased. Corey chuckled and pinched my nip, making me giggle as I swatted his hand away. "Anyway," I pressed on, "as I was trying to say, in a really BASS-ACKWARDS way, he's the reason I met you. And why I now have the perfect boyfriend and two amazing dads who love me."

Corey frowned, though his eyes stayed warm. "Um, I can think of a few thousand less extreme ways for us to have met. Like, oh, I don't know... maybe you could have just come out to your mentor? Ted could have invited you over for dinner, and we could've met over a nice home-cooked meal instead of in a 'chamber of horrors' in a creepy urology clinic. I know I would have still fallen in love with you."

I laughed. "No way! That's way too boring. Then we wouldn't have such a unique 'how we met' story."

Corey snickered into my cheek. "Aren't you the drama queen."

"Excuse you!" I shot back with feigned offense, "I prefer 'Action-Adventure Hero.'"

Corey's snicker turned into a full laugh, and then he softened. "Fine. You're amazing, either way. But seriously, Ollie, I have no idea how you can still be so positive and loving toward a man who completely betrayed you - and literally put your life in danger."

"I think it's like this: he really was a great father. Understanding, kind, supportive, and affectionate. He's the reason I'm such a hugger and lover. He was only an ass for that one day at the very end. I don't want any bad memories of him to cloud what I now have with you, Chris, and Ted. If I only focus on the good things and keep those memories alive, then I haven't really lost anything - I've just gained a new family."

Corey's expression softened into the most radiant smile. "Just three days ago, I only knew your name and how much Ted adored you. From your one meeting with Dad, even he thought you were incredible. And now, you're here - in my arms, in my bed - and you've made me the luckiest man alive. I love you, my sweet pup."

I kissed his forehead and countered with, "We're going to have to agree to disagree on that one. *I'm* the luckiest man alive."

Corey raised his head with a playful smirk. "Hey, I'm the luckiest *man* alive. You can be the luckiest *boy* - or pup. Your call."

My grin was unstoppable. "Deal! I'm your lucky pup. So... I don't suppose you want to prove how lucky we *both* are again? I believe you mentioned fun new positions?"

"Lurd, I'm in love with an insatiable 19-year-old. My balls are gonna have to start working overtime."

"Breed me again my wolf; let's make lots of puppies!"

Corey howled and I joined him. It was *Go Time* once more.

Epilogue: Our Song

Last night's storm had blown itself out, and bright sunshine streamed in through the bedroom windows. I rolled over to find Corey propped up on his elbow, watching me with a quiet reverence that made my heart flutter. His dark golden hair caught the morning light, giving him a soft, angelic halo.

And then, just like that, it happened. A song rose up in me, unbidden, impossible to resist. Before I even realized I was doing it, I sang the first line, my voice hushed and raw with the morning.

Corey's grin spread wide, and without missing a beat, he joined in, his voice blending effortlessly with mine. The words we shared, borrowed from *No Rain*, carried a simple but beautiful promise - the longing for someone to always be there, to bring comfort, to stay close through every storm. It wasn't just about avoiding sadness; it was about finding joy in the little things, about knowing that with the right person, you'll always have something beautiful to wake up to.

We finished the verse together, laughing softly at the magic of it. Corey brushed his fingers over my cheek and whispered, "Looks like we found it, pup."

Our song.